Murder Movie Club (Murder on a Monday)
(A Monthly Murder Movie Club Cozy Mystery)
By: Marcy Blesy

This book is a work of fiction. Names, characters, places, and events are a result of the imagination of the author or are used fictitiously. Any resemblance to actual persons, living or dead, businesses, events, or locations is a coincidence.

No part of the text may be reproduced without the written permission of the author, except for brief passages in reviews.

Copyright © 2025 by Marcy Blesy, LLC. All rights reserved. Cover design by Cormar Covers

The Ghost Texter Paranormal Cozy Mystery Series

Book 1
Cooking to Death (Stirring the Pot)

Book 2
Dribbling to Death (Taking His Shot)

Book 3
Haunting to Death (Taking the Wheel)
~~~~~~~~~~~~~~~~
The Tucson Valley Retirement Community Cozy Mystery Series

The books each contain a full, separate murder and can theoretically be read out of order, but the character arcs of the characters are more fully enjoyed if the books are read in order.

Book 1
Dying to Go (Nothing to Gush About)

Book 2
Dying For Wine (Seeing Red)

Book 3
Dying For Dirt (All Soaped Up)

Book 4
Dying to Build (Nailed It)

Book 5
Dying to Dance (Cha-Cha-Ahhh)

Book 6
Dying to Dink (Your Fault)

Book 7
Dying Under the Big Top (Clowning Around)

Book 8
Dying for Music (Hypnotic Harmony)

Book 9
Dying to Wed (Double Trouble)

~~~~~~~~~~~~~~~

The Monthly Murder Movie Club Cozy Mystery Series

Book 1
Murder Movie Club (Murder on a Monday)

Book 2
Murder on a Tuesday

Book 3
Murder on a Wednesday

The August Meeting of the Monthly Murder Movie Club

"No, no, no. You're wrong, Rishard. The lawyer left that note with the bartender as a clue," says April. "She wanted him to tip her off when the man who'd been in the restaurant the night of the murder showed up."

"Who do you think the man was, though, April?" asks Vicki. "The victim's former co-worker or someone we haven't met yet?" She pushes the button on the plush red movie seat and extends her legs, her favorite part of the meeting.

"I think you're both wrong," says Roberta. "I think it's the bartender himself who murdered our victim." Roberta crochets another row in the baby blanket she's making for April. She must keep her hands busy while analyzing things like plot and motive.

"Interesting idea," says Rishard. "You might be on to something."

"I know I'm right. My record stands for itself."

"But what would the bartender's motive be?" asks Yoly. She waves up at Pamela who has returned to the projector room.

"Maybe the victim owed the bartender money," says Roberta.

"Or stole his woman," adds Rishard.

"I still think we need to consider the victim's brother. He had the greatest motive," says Gladys, a summer-home owner who will be leaving the murder movie club soon.

"Alright," says Yoly, ever the leader of the little group. "It's time to fill out your cards. List your murder suspect, the weapon, and motive."

Yoly waits while everyone dutifully fills out their cards and hands their results to her. She will keep them private until the movie ends and everyone reveals their predictions. They will tally their results, and the person most correct will earn bragging rights for the month—and a small plastic trophy—which is coveted by all. In the event of an agreed-upon tie, the trophy will travel between homes throughout the month, with details of its passing to be worked out between the "winners." March was a particularly challenging month as Yoly, April, and Roberta shared a three-way tie when the neighbor's gardener used the victim's hose to strangle him because of a dispute over property lines. The reveal was less than dramatic, and the movie earned low marks, but the Monthly Murder Movie Club had a frolicking great time as usual.

    Yoly nods her head toward Pamela at the back of the movie theater. And the projector begins again.

Chapter 1

April is the first to arrive at the Northwoods Movie Theater, having dropped off the baby at her mother's house for her Monday reprieve. The only weekday with no work, and April still can't make it through the whole day with her baby alone. Seeing her daughter's desperation and impending post partem depression, April's mother had not only reluctantly volunteered to watch baby Giana, but she'd also encouraged April to join the Monthly Murder Movie Club. There's nothing further away from the freshness of a new baby than the dissection of murder mystery movies and guessing whodunits before the movie's end with like-minded people.

April smells her armpits under her sweatshirt before walking into the theater. Clean enough, she decides, though the reflection she catches of herself in the window holding a poster highlighting the current movie showing, tells her more than the slight whiff of baby formula. Bags under her eyes, knots in her scraggly blonde hair. Had she showered yesterday? Or had it been two days now? The weekend turns into one big blur of time where there is no difference between night and day as baby Giana hasn't adjusted to normal human functioning time yet. 2:00 a.m.? Sure, why not have a snack? But April is here. She'd made it through another weekend alone with the baby, the baby she never expected to have at 42, the baby she never expected to have alone after a one week stand of sweaty gymnastics in the hotel room of a local tourist. But that's another story she has no desire to dwell on.

"Let me get the door for you, young lady!" Rishard Logan reaches for the handle before April can protest. Though it's growing cool in early September, he wears his daily uniform: Hawaiian shirt and Crocs. Today it's a turquoise blue shirt with orange hibiscus flowers and coordinating orange Crocs. His remaining gray hair shimmers under the bright sun that falls over northern Michigan this afternoon.

"Thanks, Rishard."

"How's that cute baby girl?" he grins.

"She's growing like a weed, almost six months now."

"Oh boy. Before you know it, she'll be crawling. You'd better baby proof if you haven't yet. I remember when my son started walking. We had to take out our kitchen chairs for a full year. He was quite a crawler." Rishard laughs. "Of course, that was thirty years ago. He's thirty-eight and raising his own little rascals now."

"Right, I'll add babyproofing to my list of things to do," April says dryly, blowing a loose strand of hair out of her face. She wonders if there is an end to the list of parenting or if it's an unattainable goal that's designed to make one feel inferior with every decision made since it can never be completed.

The lobby lights are dim when the two unlikely friends enter, not the usual bright lights above the concession stand. The popcorn machine sits empty, the free smells of butter and salt missing. It's not unusual that crowds of people aren't jockeying for their tickets to the Monday afternoon matinee. For one thing, the tourists who flock to Northwoods for summer fun in northern Michigan every summer have gone home. There will be fall leaf enthusiasts arriving soon, but nothing matches the energy of the summer crowd in a lake town. Plus, the fall visitors are more transient and don't look for things to do on a regular basis like those with a second home in Northwoods. And since the manager of the Northwoods Theater created the Monthly Murder Movie Club, only serious murder mystery fans show up anyway. Most people don't like the movie to be stopped in the middle to allow the audience to discuss their theories and make predictions as to the murderer. But it's this very premise that brings the few viewers together every month—less now than in August—but still a solid core of people with a shared interest in solving mysteries. What the Monthly Murder Movie Club *didn't* expect this Monday afternoon, is that they'd be thrown into the middle of an *actual* murder.

Chapter 2

"Scandal! Scandal! Scandal!" Roberta Kato yells over and over in the lobby of the movie theater. It's not particularly alarming for April and Rishard to hear Roberta yelling her trademark word. She's often heard yelling it right before break time in the middle of their Monday murder mysteries—her way of letting the others think she's solved the movie's murder. It's Vicki's cue to call *Action,* and Pamela shuts off the movie projector while the audience members gather in the middle of the theater to discuss the possible motives and suspects for the on-screen murder. But the movie hasn't started. And no one is even in the theater.

"What's she carrying on about?" asks Vicki, who has arrived and is following April and Rishard toward the sound of Roberta's high-pitched voice.

Rishard and April ignore Vicki, though April sneezes three times in rapid succession, overcome by Vicki's perfume. She wonders how Vicki's clients in her beauty shop can stand to spend an hour in close proximity. She has to sit at least a row away from her just to breathe normally.

Roberta's eyes are wide as she stands over the body that is lying in front of the concession stand counter, face down but still identifiable. The soles of Roberta's shoes flash neon colors as she jumps up and down, activating the sensors with her quick movement. "It's Junior Cash!" she yells, straddling the back of poor Junior's body as she reaches down to feel for a pulse on his neck.

"Oh my goodness!" says April.

"What's the call, Roberta?" asks Rishard.

"Isn't it obvious?" asks Vicki. "He's dead! Our poor, young John E. Cash is dead!" She throws her hands in front of her face and begins to wail.

Roberta whips her head around faster than a poor calf being lassoed at the rodeo and jumps back toward the concession stand. "The least you could do, Vicki, is honor the man's request to be called Junior. The poor soul hated being called by his given name, and I can't say that I blame him. Johnny Cash is so 1968." Roberta shakes her head back and forth as if the discussion of Junior Cash's name is more important than the fact that he's lying dead on the floor.

"Don't touch anything!" yells April, ever the pragmatist.

"Why, honey?" asks Vicki. "He's clearly had a medical condition. There's no sign of something bad happenin' to our sweet Junior.

"I wouldn't be so quick to make that judgment, Vicki." Rishard points to a red liquid that is slowly flowing from underneath the center of Junior's body.

Rather than going around the back of the concession stand, Roberta hops the counter with her springy shoes helping her five foot stature accomplish this feat. "What are you doing?" asks April, hugging her body tightly with her arms as she passes her gaze between Junior and Roberta. Vicki takes out a blue handkerchief from her purse and drapes it over the back of Junior's head.

April snatches the handkerchief and balls it up in frustration. "I said don't touch anything! That includes putting anything *on* Junior, too! You act like you've never see a murder mystery movie!"

"That's mean, April," says Vicki who holds out her hand for April to return the handkerchief. "My mother made that for me and gave it to me on my sixteenth birthday. You act as if I am—"

"Ladies, stop arguing!" yells Rishard, often irritated as the only male voice in the Monthly Murder Movie Club. "What is it, Roberta? What are you doing back there?"

Roberta holds up her empty hands and waves them around in the air. "It's gone," she says quietly, an uncharacteristic quality from Roberta.

"What's gone, Roberta?" asks April.

"Junior's knife."

"Junior had a knife?" asks Vicki.

Roberta nods her head up and down quickly. "He showed it to me once, after a disgruntled patron threatened to clean out his concession stand by smashing the counter with a baseball bat. That shook Junior up, so he brought in his dad's old Swiss Army knife—"

"The kind with tools like a screwdriver and a nail file?" asks April. "That doesn't sound too intimidating."

"You're right. But that was Junior. He thought he could protect himself more with his words than with any weapon. It certainly wasn't the kind of knife like the one I carried with me in Vietnam."

Rishard looks side-eyed at Vicki and April as if to say, *here she goes again with her talk of serving in Vietnam,* but now is not the time to discuss the merits of Roberta's recollection of the past.

"Oh my kooky koalas!" Vicki points across the room to the display for this week's movie, a cardboard cutout of

Dane Dimoli, the star in the *Murder Meets Michigan* movie about a serial killer that everyone was to be watching right now. And through Dane's heart is a knife—a bloody knife—and it's not a Swiss Army knife.

Chapter 3

"Don't touch anything!" April yells again.

"We know. We know," says Roberta who has reached into her *Beach Life* bag. She pulls out yellow caution tape and drapes it around anything she can find nearby from the popcorn machine to the ticket booth counter to Dane Dimoli himself.

"Why do you have caution tape in your purse?" asks Vicki.

"One can never be too prepared for murder." A line of spit leaves Roberta's mouth as she says Vicki's name, an undertone of animosity between the two women that is never far away.

April pulls out her phone and punches in the numbers for 911. "What are you doing, April?" Rishard pushes the red button before April can complete her call. "This is an opportunity that doesn't come around every day! Let's play this out, do our own investigation before we call the police." He winks at April who melts a little bit in his presence, like the dad she always wanted and never knew. Plus, April never did have much good judgment when it came to deferring to men, though Rishard means no harm. "There's nothing worse coming to Junior. We came here to discuss murder, so if that's what's going on, we have a lot to talk about."

"I am so sorry I was late!" A tall woman with a baseball hat rushes into the lobby of the Northwoods Movie Theater. She has a bag of cookies in her hand. Though the concession stand treats satiate everyone at the theater, the Monthly Murder Movie Club created a calendar for homemade snacks a long time ago—*something to make this day stand out a little more than the typical visit to the theater,* Rishard had said. But Rishard needs no excuses to eat more than popcorn and boxed candy. Ever since his last divorce—his fourth—he relishes in the homemade treats of the women he gathers with once a month. "Why aren't you watching the movie?"

"Hello, Yoly. We're a bit distracted by the murder mystery unfolding in the lobby at the moment," says Rishard.

"Murder mystery?" Yoly cocks her head to the side as her eyes pan from Rishard to Roberta behind the counter to Vicki with thick smeared eyeliner raining down her face, to April who hovers her fingers over her phone. Then her eyes fall to the ground. "Junior!"

Yoly drops her bag of cookies and rushes to Junior's side, but April puts a hand on her arm and pulls her back to her feet. "Don't touch anything!" she says for the third time today.

"What happened?" Yoly asks.

April points to the cutout of Dane Dimoli with the bloody knife through his cardboard heart. She can't help smiling as it seems somehow fitting that the debonair man with a reputation for collecting women like a stamp collector collects stamps should have a knife pierced through his likeness.

"Why are you smilin', April?" asks Vicki. As she shakes her head in disapproval, her large, teased hair hits Rishard in the face, and he begins to cough.

"How much hairspray do you have in the football helmet?" he asks as he points to Vicki's head.

"Oof," says Roberta who has now hopped up onto the counter and is dangling her little legs over the edge. For 75, Roberta is quite limber.

Vicki squints her eyes as she looks Rishard up and down. "How dare a man in a Hawaiian shirt and Crocs insult my perfectly styled hair?"

"Hey, maybe we should discuss the most pressing matter in the room," says April, as she checks her watch, keenly aware of how much time she has free before she has to pick up Giana. Grandma of the Year is not an award April will ever bestow upon her mother.

"Right. I'll take notes," says Roberta. She pulls out a notebook and pen from her massive bag. But before she begins to write anything down, she also pulls out an Army dress hat, the kind one might wear when attending a fancy military ball, not to wear into battle. Roberta always puts on the hat she claims was hers from Vietnam when conjecturing about the suspects and motives of the Monday movies. Then Pamela would restart the movie, and they'd watch their guesses come true or implode on the screen. Rishard takes great offense to Roberta's hat, not convinced she'd ever been in the US military—let alone seen combat in Vietnam—possibly because his own father had fled to Canada during the 60s to avoid the draft, and Rishard held some sort of embarrassment.

"Let's start with what we know," says Yoly, her former school principal experience providing the direction that's needed right now. She straightens the University of Michigan baseball hat on her head, never one for any more primping than light lip gloss and a clean hat over her short brown hair, not for lack of Vicki offering her guidance. "When did you notice Junior's body?" she asks.

"April and I walked in at 12:50. I held the door, so she walked in first." He hits his chest as if everyone should be pleased with his chivalry. "But we weren't the first ones here."

"It's true," says Roberta. "I arrived a few minutes before. Junior wasn't at the ticket counter, so I didn't know what to do. Junior is *always* at the ticket counter before he moves to the concession stand, of course."

"Of course," says Vicki. "Junior has proven himself to be reliable, especially when Pamela's on vacation. Do you remember last year when Pamela left Junior in charge of the theater for the first time, though? She called each one of us after movie club to make sure that Junior shut off the popcorn machine and locked up."

"I remember that!" says Rishard. "I had to leave a perfectly lovely dinner date early to come back and rattle the doors."

"Were they locked?" April asks.

"Absolutely. I tried to reach my date and ask for a nightcap, but she ghosted me, as you young people say." Rishard looks at April.

"I can relate," she says only loud enough for Rishard to hear. He pats her on the top of the head like she were a pathetic puppy.

"Someone should call Pamela."

"Let's focus, team!" says Yoly. "Roberta, when you arrived, other than Junior not being at the ticket counter, did you notice anything else unusual?"

"I sure did." Roberta straightens her hat which makes Rishard grunt in irritation. "The smell."

"What about the smell?" asks the woman who smells like the counter at Macy's.

"Vicki, it was the *lack* of smell I should have said. There was no popcorn." She points at the machine behind her.

"That is odd," says April. "Junior takes great pride in his popcorn." Everyone nods their head in agreement.

"And then, of course, the fact that Junior was lying face down in front of the counter was odd," says Roberta who appears to write that most obvious observation down in her notebook.

April rolls her eyes, annoyed by the seniorist senior in this group of seniors. Her mother might be right in pointing out the fact that April spends more time with people over 50 than anyone closer in age to her at the ripe old age of 42. Something about this quirky group of pre-seniors—as Yoly likes to refer to herself—and actual AARP members can be oddly comforting. But at the same time, their nonchalant discussion about an *actual* murder before them has her rattled.

"Write down the bloody knife through Dane's cardboard heart!" says Vicki.

"And the pool of blood by Junior's body," says Rishard.

"Scandal! Scandal! Look at the blood!" shrieks Roberta, lifting her legs and sitting cross-legged on the counter now. "His blood is spreading."

"Which means it's fresh," says Rishard.

"So, he was recently killed," says April.

"Did you see anyone leaving when you all arrived?" asks Yoly. Rishard, April, and Roberta shake their heads as they widen their eyes in shared understanding. "The killer may still be in the building."

Chapter 4

"Rishard! Check the men's room in the basement!" says Yoly, taking control once more. "April, you take the ladies' room downstairs. Vicki, assess the family bathroom down the hall. Roberta, check the theater."

No one moves a muscle. "And what exactly are you going to do, Yoly?" asks Rishard. A tuft of white hair peeks through the unbuttoned top of his shirt, not at all endearing him to any of the ladies as he wishes.

"Me? I'm going to stand right here and make sure the murderer doesn't run out the front door. *Someone* has to watch the front door."

"What about the exit from the front of the theater?" asks April. "Our suspect could very easily have slipped through that door and be long gone by now."

"I suppose that's possible," says Yoly.

"That's what I would have done if I'd killed Junior," says Roberta. Everyone stares at her for a beat too long. "What? I didn't say I *did* kill him."

"You *were* the only one here when we first arrived," says Rishard.

"Are you suggesting that I killed Junior, knowing full well that my clubmates would be arriving as fresh blood poured from his body? Do you think I'd be that careless?" As she shakes her head in disgust, her military hat falls off and lands at Rishard's feet. He does not pick it up.

April chews on the inside of her cheek as she looks uneasily between Roberta and Junior who hasn't moved a lick since his death. "What are you thinkin', dear?" asks Vicki, patting her arm.

"It's probably nothing," she says, looking at Roberta one more time before looking up at the ceiling.

"Spit it out, woman," says Roberta who jumps off the counter and marches up to April, her shoes flashing neon with every sharp step until she stops in front of her, looking up to meet her gaze.

April takes a step back. Roberta takes a step forward. Rishard moves between the two women, youngest and oldest of the group, a bodyguard of sorts. "Fine. I'll say it." April straightens her shoulders and extends her body with her posture. She wants to be heard. She's tired of being defined as the woman who let a perfect stranger impregnate her in a night of drunken passion. She's tired of receiving the group's judgment. Their pity, too. Truthfully, she's just tired of being tired. "I heard you threaten Pamela last month, after the movie."

"Threaten Pamela? That's absurd," says Roberta.

"What did you hear, April?" asks Yoly.

"You were furious that your whodunit guess was wrong for three months in a row. You told Pamela that you'd ruin her 'little theater' if she didn't start choosing movie mysteries with more realistic plots."

"Oh, for scandal's sake. I meant that I'd tell everyone to avoid Northwoods Theater. Maybe I'd tell them that I heard that there were lice living in the seats or that the carpets had mold. I didn't mean that I'd kill her ticket-taking popcorn maker. Are you insane?" Roberta stomps across the room. She pulls out her cellphone and begins taking close-up pictures of the knife in Dane Dimoli's body.

"Roberta wouldn't kill anyone. She doesn't have it in her," says Rishard.

"I heard that!" she yells. "I've killed lots of people—in war—whether you believe me or not."

"Sure you did, Roberta. Sure you did."

"Well, if Roberta didn't kill Junior, then who do you think did?" asks Vicki.

"Maybe the lad had a disgruntled girlfriend," says Rishard. "Goodness knows, I've angered a lady or two." Vicki wrinkles her nose.

"I hear a lot of gossip at my shop, you know, people sitting in my revolvin' chair all day long every day—except for Mondays, obviously. And people like to talk." Vicki touches her hair as if to make sure it's still there, and it doesn't move a strand.

"You mean, more like *you* can't stop asking for information," Roberta says, sneering at Vicki as she appears to be checking the perimeter of the room looking for something.

"I can't help it that people find me a safe person to talk to. Some of us have that kind of charm, unlike *others*," she says as she meets Roberta's gaze to which Roberta appears to gather spit in her mouth out of anger.

"Roberta! Gross! Stop it!" says April, stopping Roberta from acting out and taking a step back toward the counter where she knocks over a display of candy boxes.

"Go on, Vicki. What information did you learn about Junior at the salon?" asks Yoly.

"Junior grew up in Northwoods. I used to cut his mom's hair before she passed when he was in middle school. It was a really sad story. Poor kid. She slipped on a trail in the UP and didn't recover. So much beauty there, and so much danger if you're not payin' attention to what you're doin'." Everyone nods along with her story, even Roberta who has rejoined the group. "His daddy raised him as best he could, but John G. Cash was a homely man."

"What's being homely got to do with how he raised his kid?" asks Rishard. "From what I remember of the senior John Cash, he ran the local diner in town and employed his son. Seems like he was trying the best he could to earn money and still keep watch over his kid. Sounds like good parenting to me."

"I suppose that's not an important part of the story," agrees Vicki. "Junior got his mama's looks—thank goodness—but he also got his daddy's work ethic."

"That sounds like a great combination to me," says Yoly. "Junior attended Northwoods High School when I was principal. He was one of those kids who blended in, didn't stand out for any reason really, good or bad. He stayed quiet, did his schoolwork, had a couple of friends. Nothing that *I* remember about Junior Cash screams, *murder me!*"

"That's because you don't know how to get the good gossip like I do." Vicki raises her eyebrows and winks at no one in particular. She begins to whisper as if outsiders will hear her words, but everyone leans in closer nonetheless. "I heard from Mel Thompson who heard from her niece Katie who heard from her boyfriend Wally that Junior might have been dealing with the illegals."

"The illegals?" asks April, wrinkling her nose in genuine confusion.

"The drugs," Vicki says.

"What kind of drugs?" asks Roberta. "You know that marijuana is legal now in Michigan, not that I have any firsthand knowledge."

Vicki grunts out loud while Rishard rolls his eyes because everyone knows about Roberta's extracurricular activities. To each their own. "I'm not sure. I'm not a detective, just a hairdresser."

"Speaking of detective, I think it's time to call the police. Whatever the cause of Junior's death, the longer he lays here on the floor of the lobby, the longer his killer runs free," says April. "Plus, I need to pick up the baby soon. We can't do anything to help Junior now."

"I think we can," says Roberta. "Who better to solve the murder of our ticket-taking, popcorn-making friend than the Monthly Murder Movie Club? We come here every month to *literally* try to solve a murder—"

"But on-screen," says April.

"Right, on-screen. But today we got something better. Rest in peace and all that, of course. Today we got a *real murder*. We're smart people. Let's put our sleuthing hats on and figure this out ourselves." Roberta straightens her own hat that's gone askew again with all of her snooping around the room.

"We can't just leave poor Junior on the floor," says Yoly. "We *have* to call the police."

"Fine, but let's take a thorough inventory of the place first, get a leg up. You know how slow the Northwoods Police can be at solving a crime.

"It's true," says Vicki. "It took three months before they figured out who was spray painting the salon's front window with curse words!"

"Those weren't curse words, Vicki," says Rishard. "Those were coupon codes for Big Ted's Carwash."

"Well, the point is," says Roberta, "we may be able to solve this murder faster than the police."

At that moment, the sound of footsteps running up the aisle from inside the theater causes everyone to scatter and hide: April and Rishard behind the counter. Vicki and Yoly inside the ticket booth. And Roberta? Behind Dane Dimoli.

Chapter 5

"Come back! Angela, come back!" A man's voice yells the same thing repeatedly as the sound of his footsteps get closer to the door between the theater and the lobby. April puts her right hand on Rishard's back as they crouch on the floor next to the scattered candy from the counter display. She says a small prayer that she'll see her daughter again, feeling strongly guilty for ever wishing that she weren't a mother. And now she might never get to be one again if a murderer is rushing into the lobby to add to his victim count.

"Ahhhh! Ouch! Ouch! Her nails! Get her off me!" Vicki screams from inside the ticket booth.

"Noah?" says Roberta as she steps out from behind cardboard Dane. "What are you doing here? You don't usually clean up until the movie's over." She looks at her large watch. "And we're supposed to have another hour."

"I know. Ugh. I know! I came into town early to do some shopping. My girlfriend's birthday is this weekend, so I wanted to pick her out something real special at the jewelry store down the street. It's kind of a new relationship to be buying jewelry, but I'm trying to impress her. Working as a janitor in a movie theater isn't the most grand job. Go figure."

April and Rishard stand up from behind the counter. April waves shyly at the good-looking janitor who'd agreed to come in on his one day off to clean up after the Monthly Murder Movie Club. "Hello, Noah. Nice to see you."

"Hi, Rishard. April."

"Someone get this cat out of here!" Vicki has pulled herself up to the ticket counter in the booth. She looks like a mannequin in a store window, but anyone who might be walking by right now would surely run the other direction rather than patronize this business. She looks terrified and also comical as her helmet hair presses against the top of the booth.

Yoly leans over the bottom of the Dutch door that remains closed as she passes off a large tabby cat named Angela. The cat is wearing a red bow tie and acting quite self-important.

Noah takes ownership of the naughty cat and proceeds to deposit her in a cat carrier that sits just inside the theater for moments of escape from Pamela's office that happen often with Angela. "This cat will be the death of me. If I didn't know that Pamela loved her more than any other living being, I'd have recommended her swift delivery to a farm." He growls which makes the cat growl back.

"Did Angela make it outside?" asks Rishard.

"She sure did. I was just coming out of the jewelry store when I saw her licking her paws on a bench between Priscilla's Pretzels and the Unsalted, No Sharks T-shirt Shop. She hadn't a care in the world. I thought it'd be an easy retrieval. Scoop her up, use my key to come in through the theater door, and put her back in Pamela's office. WRONG! She started running the second I saw her. But she's not as bright as she lets on because she ran straight back to the theater."

"Wait a second," says April who has begun to pick up the spilled boxes of candy. "Why is Angela in Pamela's office if she's on vacation?"

"Pamela told me that she'd tried boarding Angela in the past, but surprise surprise, that mean cat doesn't play well with others. She asked Junior to check in on her a few times a day. I guess he didn't close her office door tightly. You'd have to ask Junior."

"Yeah, that's not going to be possible," says Roberta who marches over to Junior's body that lies just out of view from where Noah stands. "Say, Noah, you wouldn't happen to know anything about this, uh, situation, would you?"

"What situ…oh my…oh no…is he…is he—"

"Deader than a racoon on a country road," says Roberta.

"Roberta, have some respect!" says April. "Hey! What's this key for?" April holds up a key that had been underneath a box of M&M's.

"It's probably Junior's key," says Yoly who, along with Vicki, has exited the ticket booth. Vicki's hair stands up in places not intended when she prepared to go out into the world this morning, and no one can stop staring at her until Noah speaks.

"I have no idea how you all are staying so calm." Noah sucks in his breath and exhales slowly. Can someone please tell me what happened?"

"It's pretty obvious, son. Someone drove a knife through his chest," says Rishard.

"I…what?"

Yoly puts a comforting hand on his arm. "Take a minute. Not everyone's as familiar with murder as we are."

Noah nods his head but doesn't say anything.

"Can we get back to the key now?" asks Roberta. "Did Junior lose his key?"

April runs her fingers over the notches of the key as she contemplates someone using Junior's own key to let him or her into the theater only to kill Junior when he arrived. But that doesn't make much sense to her, as Junior would have needed the key to let *himself* in.

"Nah, Junior always wore his key around his neck on a chain his mom gave him as a child. It was kind of sweet. I don't think that key belongs to Junior." Noah leans back against the candy counter for support. He's so close, April could wrap her arms around him. She blushes with embarrassment and dismisses her thoughts as post-pregnancy hormones run amok.

"Hmm…" says Roberta.

"Don't touch him!" yells April, knowing exactly what she's thinking.

"Just a real quick peek. I already checked his neck for his pulse, so the police will understand." Roberta crouches low next to Junior's body but is careful to avoid the side where his blood has been pooling. She touches the collar of his button-down shirt and lifts it up. The Monthly Murder Movie Club members lean over Junior's body as Roberta carefully twists a gold chain from the front of Junior's neck to the back. Sure enough, a key hangs on the chain.

April holds up the key in her hand. "Looks pretty similar to me," she says. "Maybe there was an extra stored under the counter, and one of us knocked it down. With all this moving around in here today, it's possible."

"I don't think so," says Noah. "Pamela took account of who had access to the theater. It's her pride and joy, after all. I'm pretty confident that only Junior, Pamela, and I had keys to the building."

"Another mystery," says Yoly.

"Another mystery," everyone repeats, followed by a howl from Angela inside the carrier, clearly distressed by her predicament.

"Someone's gonna have to take that cat," says Noah. "I'm sure as heck not touching her again."

"I can't take her. I have a baby!" says April, the next to bail.

"Clearly, Angela and I do not get along," says Vicki as she tries to ply her fingers through the out-of-place strands of over-hair sprayed hair.

Yoly, Rishard, and Roberta stare at each other, waiting for a volunteer. Roberta breaks first. "Ah, fine! I'll take the wretched animal. My mother tolerates cats."

"Your mother?" asks Noah. "Uh, no offense. It's just that I didn't assume that, well—"

"I'll save you from yourself, Noah," says April, smiling at the sweet man who's burying himself into a hole with his words. Why must all the good ones be taken, she muses in her mind. "Roberta's mother is 97 and lives with her in a condo that overlooks Lake Michigan."

"It's a rocking home, Noah. You should be so lucky one day."

"That sounds real nice, Ms. Roberta. I hope I didn't offend you."

"You did offend me, Noah, but I have thick skin, what with my war experience and all."

"Here we go again," says Rishard, throwing up his hands in frustration.

"Roberta," says Yoly, "Angela's a fighter, not a lap cat. Are you sure she should be around your mother?"

"Mamo's a fighter, too. Angela's the one that should be afraid."

Chapter 6

Officers Clarence Cleary and Bethany Spelling arrive on the scene an hour and a half after the body was discovered by Roberta Kato and the others in the Monthly Murder Movie Club. The timeline's fudged a bit with the quiet understanding of all in attendance, including Noah, that nothing more could have been done for poor Junior Cash. No harm. No foul. At least that's what they tell themselves. Truthfully, everyone's frustrated that they'd settled on calling in the police without getting a better look around the theater, but April had to pick up her baby.

"So, let me get this straight. You arrived for your murder club?" asks Officer Cleary, a large man with shifty eyes and a hovering stature that can make one feel small and confess to crimes that they did not commit, but Roberta is standing strong with her story.

"That's right, officer. I'm a veteran." She points to her hat. "Do you think that maybe you could allow some professional courtesy here? Maybe *believe me* instead of interrogating me like *I'm* the one who's committed this dastardly crime."

"Thank you for your service, ma'am," says Officer Spelling, a large woman in her own right with broad shoulders and a tight bun of black hair on top of her head. Her demeanor is the good cop to Officer Cleary's bad cop persona. Rishard mutters something under his breath, but everyone ignores him. No sense in delving into the conspiracy theory that Rishard has created in his mind that Roberta is simply *pretending* to be a veteran to garner admiration from others. "We're just trying to understand the timeline. Someone with your…uh, experience, can surely understand that."

"Right. Of course I can."

"Hold on a minute," Officer Cleary says to Roberta and his partner. "I'm questioning something called a *murder club*. That's what I need help understanding at this moment."

April, Rishard, Yoly, Vicki, and Roberta share a knowing look before beginning to giggle. Rishard fixes the confusion by putting a hand on the shoulder of Officer Cleary who *clearly* does not appreciate being touched as he steps back so quickly that he trips over poor Junior's shoes and lands on his butt right under the sign that's flashing the Northwoods Theater's marquee outside.

"It was the manager of the theater's idea to bring in different groups of movie goers on a regular basis. Once a month, on a Monday, a group of people attend a viewing of a murder mystery movie. Then, about halfway through, after all of the potential suspects have made their appearances in the movie, Pamela or Junior stop the projector," says Rishard. "Pamela's the manager."

"Then we gather together in the middle of the theater and compare notes," says Vicki, not able to stop herself from butting into Rishard's explanation.

"They get quite animated in their discussions," says Noah. "I sometimes arrive before my shift starts just to hear them squabble." Noah catches April's eye, and they share a sweet smile. No one else seems to notice.

"Interesting marketing plan," says Officer Cleary.

"Brilliant really," says Roberta.

"Hmm. And where is Pamela today?" asks Officer Spelling. Her question sounds accusatory, but she's still smiling.

"Vacation. She always takes time off between the end of the summer tourist season and the fall leaf viewing season," says Yoly. She points to her sweatshirt that says *Beachin' in Northwoods*. "The locals need trips, too."

"Seems convenient," says Officer Cleary, showing some shade. "Does anyone know where she might be located?" he asks.

A shrug of shoulders provides the answer. "I have an emergency number if you'd like it. Pamela's pretty private about her personal life," says Noah.

"Yes, I think I need that number. Thanks. Now, back to Mr. Cash—"

"Junior," says Roberta. "He hated his given name."

"That's right. Remember when we brought him to the station a month ago, boss? He jumped down your throat when you called him John Cash." Officer Spelling looks at Officer Cleary who nods in remembrance. Vicki looks at Roberta who looks at Rishard who looks at April, all with raised eyebrows. "I'd like to know who found the body."

"All of us!" shouts Roberta before anyone else can answer with the truth. "We arrived at the same time, 1:00 sharp for our matinee showing. But Noah came later. He found Angela outside wandering the streets and brought her in. She's quite a little devil, that one."

"Angela?" Officer Spelling narrows her eyes and looks around the room as if trying to find the cantankerous Angela but probably expecting to find a woman. At that moment, the ornery cat lets out an ear-piercing meow from the cat carrier at the feet of Noah, causing the officers to startle.

"That's Angela," says Yoly. 'She belongs to Pamela. You know, *Pam and Angela* from *The Office*? Pamela's a huge fan. And I can say very confidently that both of them live up to their characters' personas, especially Angela." Yoly shudders and wags her finger at Angela who pays her no notice. She only wants free.

"Does the cat live in the theater?" Officer Cleary sneezes loudly. "Sorry. I'm highly allergic to cats."

"Oof, that's not good," says Rishard. "Angela has very long fur for a tabby cat. You'd better ask your questions quickly."

"Right." Officer Cleary looks at his notepad. "You *all* arrived at 1:00 *sharp* except for Noah who came later with the cat. Did any of you touch anything?"

Another succession of shared looks passes around the lobby. Everyone shakes their head except for Roberta who acknowledges that she checked for Junior's pulse on his neck.

"That's a sensible thing to do. Thank you. Anything else you might find helpful to offer? Any ideas about why someone might want to harm Mr. Cas…Junior?" he asks.

"Nope."

"Can't think of anything."

"Everything seems fine here." No one in the Monthly Murder Movie Club wishes to share a theory. A silent collective decision to solve this mystery for themselves has been decided. What a wondrous opportunity for a murder club to try to solve a *real* murder!

"Does anyone have an explanation for the crime tape?" Officer Cleary points to Roberta's tape which she has draped around the room.

"That's just our usual Monthly Murder Movie Club décor, kind of like streamers," Roberta lies.

"Uh-huh. And what about a murder weapon?" asks Officer Cleary as he stares at the puddle of blood coming from the middle of Junior's body.

"It's in the cardboard cut—" begins April until Roberta stomps on her foot. Only Vicki, Yoly, and Rishard notice as Roberta's shoes illuminate along the edge.

"Nope," says Roberta. "No weapon that we know of."

"Are you sure?" Officer Spelling asks April directly.

"Nope. I don't know a thing. But you can see on the movie poster from what was supposed to be today's viewing of *Murder Meets Michigan* that the weapon was a meat cleaver. Can you imagine?" April hopes that she's hiding her nervousness from the officers, but everyone in the Monthly Murder Movie Club recognizes her uneasiness as she stares across the room.

Because the knife through Dane Dimoli's heart is gone.

Chapter 7

When the Monthly Murder Movie Club has been released, they reassemble in the alleyway between Rustic Charm Antiques and Delish in Northwoods, the local bakery. Roberta's having a hard time maintaining control of Angela's cat carrier as the pesky pet won't stop moving.

"Maybe she's really hungry," offers Yoly.

Roberta raises her shoulders. "Well, she'd better like chicken and rice because that's what I've got in the crockpot."

"I don't think it's a good idea to feed human food to cats," says Yoly. "My sister-in-law's a veterinarian and always giving her kids a hard time when they feed scraps to their dog."

"Maybe your sister-in-law should kick out her grown children, and then she wouldn't have that problem," says Vicki. "Tsk, tsk, kids these days stay far too long in their parents' homes." She shivers as a light breeze blows through the alleyway. "I need to get home and reset this hair. I'm a mess. What's the plan?"

"I think we should meet on Wednesday, somewhere private. That will give us a few days to do some detective work. Roberta, can I see your notebook since you're a little occupied there?" Yoly points to the notebook that's sticking out of her bag.

"Suit yourself."

Yoly reaches for the notebook and reads through Roberta's notes. "If you are going to be our official note taker, you really need to work on your penmanship."

Roberta holds out the cat carrier. "Would you care to take Angela off my hands so that I can practice my handwriting, Principal Yoly?" she says full of sweet saccharin.

"I believe I can make out your notes." Yoly clears her throat and reads through Roberta's chicken scratches. Leave it to a former teacher and principal to be able to make sense of the worst penmanship. "Okay, I think I have this figured out. Vicki, can you use your sources to investigate the drug angle, to see if Junior perhaps angered someone he purchased drugs from?"

"Or sold drugs *to*," says Vicki. "Yes, I can do that."

"Great. And, Rishard, how comfortable are you talking to Junior's dad, after the police contact him first, naturally? I suppose he's going to receive a great shock."

"I have great empathy."

"Maybe don't wear something so cheery and colorful with hibiscus flowers?" says Roberta.

"I can handle my own fashion, Roberta. Maybe you should consider representing your attire accurately and quit trying to gain respect for something you never did?"

Roberta sets Angela's cat carrier onto the ground, barely missing Rishard's Croc-covered foot. "Listen here, *Richard!*"

"It's *Rishard,* and you know that!"

"Friends, *friends,* don't blow this chance. The MONTHLY MURDER MOVIE CLUB has a chance to solve a *real* murder. Don't screw it up by squabbling!" says Yoly. Rishard and Roberta exchange glares but refrain from further communication. "Good. That's better. I'll recollect my memories from his time in school to see if I can unlock anything that might help our case. April, I know it's hard with the baby. Don't worry about anything, dear."

"No, it's fine! I still have the key. I can visit the hardware store and see if it's a recent copy. I was thinking about calling Noah and picking his brain a bit further."

"Oh yes," says Yoly.

"Wonderful idea," says Rishard.

"That's fantastic!" says Vicki.

"Good choice. Finally, a good choice," adds Roberta.

April's quite confused by their reactions, wondering if they think her incompetent because of her recent predicament. What she doesn't realize is that they've hoped for a Noah and April union ever since they first started meeting eight months ago when April was still bursting with Giana. But now is not the time to tell her their secret desires. Plus, Noah has just bought jewelry for his new girlfriend.

"And that brings us to Roberta." Everyone turns to stare, giving their best condemning looks. "The knife? What in the name of all things sacred do you plan on doing with the *murder weapon?*"

"Shh! Not so loud, Yoly. Do you want everyone in Northwoods knowing about the murder in our small town?"

"They are going to know very soon. Nothing stays quiet in a small town," says Rishard.

"Exactly," says Roberta. "No one will know about the knife—except for us and the killer, of course—at least not that it was *this kind of knife*. She uses a tissue to pull the blood-covered knife from an empty makeup bag inside her *Beach Life* bag. The ornate handle looks to be engraved as it's the first close-up inspection anyone has made aside from Roberta. But this is not the place to investigate further.

"Put that away!" says April.

"Oh my word!" Vicki clutches her chest.

"You are going to be in so much trouble if Officer Cleary finds out that you took the murder weapon," says Rishard.

"Not when we solve the murder before the Northwoods Police Department. Think about it. It's *our* chance to figure this out ourselves. How fun will this be? Plus, I didn't touch it with my bare hands. I'm not that stupid. I used a tissue in case there are fingerprints that the police can check for *later*."

Yoly takes a slow deep breath. "Two days. I will give you two days until our next meeting to come to a conclusion before we turn that in. *Two days*. Do you understand?"

Roberta shrugs her shoulders. "Maybe three or four days. But don't worry about a thing. I'll see you all at April's apartment on Wednesday."

April stands up a little taller at the mention of her name. "My apartment?"

"Of course, silly," says Vicki. "We all know what it's like to have little kids. We'll come to you. Don't worry about a thing."

"Right. Uh-huh. That sounds great." But nothing about that idea sounds great to April.

Chapter 8

Yoly enters her house on First Street in Northwoods, in the Old West neighborhood. It's full of cobblestone streets and houses built in the early 1900s. Yoly lives in one of those houses, a two-story colonial with symmetrical designs and a large front porch. It's not the fanciest house on the street. But, then again, retired principals never earned enough in their career to live in houses like those across the streets with fancy columns, second-story porches, and bricklain sidewalks leading to the back of the house. Yoly doesn't even have a garage, but it's never caused more of a problem than the extra time needed to remove snow. Unless you count the time that Snyder Collins poured sugar in her gas tank after he'd been given Saturday detention the weekend of the Holiday Basketball Tournament after he'd cheated on a test. But they don't even have Saturday detentions anymore. Kids are too soft these days—and their parents, too—thinks Yoly often about today's youth.

There is no Mr. attached to Yoly anymore. She divorced the second husband two years ago, the year she'd retired. She got rid of the job *and* the husband. What a rebirth it had felt like at the time, until the sewer backed up (old house problems). And then there'd been a small electrical fire in the attic that had led to new plumbing *and* new electrical at the same time, and she'd wished for a husband to calm her nerves and help pay for the messes. She's persevered, however, and here she is now, leading a murder mystery club—at least she still fancies herself a leader—and solving an actual murder in real time. Poor Junior. He didn't deserve to end up on the wrong end of that knife.

    Yoly takes off her baseball cap and hangs it on her hat rack which holds only two hats, her University of Michigan baseball cap and a Detroit Red Wings winter hat. She heats up water in the microwave with a jasmine tea bag and turns on her laptop. She considers herself a techy person, not yet old enough at 56 to use age to swear off technology like Roberta or Vicki, though Vicki's only a few years older. What Northwoods School District doesn't know is that Yoly maintains her password into the school's database of past students. She can't access any students entered into the district after she retired, but she can—and often does—take a peek at the records of past students. It thrills her immensely to reminisce about days gone by, trouble made, successes earned, scandals hidden within some of those records. Yoly doesn't miss the day-to-day grind, but she misses her students and even some of her staff.

"What do you think, Larry? What secrets did John E. Cash carry?" Yoly pats the top of Larry's urn before sitting down at her kitchen table to delve into the school records. Larry was the one who got away, literally. He'd gone on a hiking trip with his brothers to the Andes Mountains and gotten lost after a squabble with them. Leave it to Larry to think he could handle things better on his own. He couldn't. And he didn't. Now he sits in an urn in the middle of Yoly's kitchen table, the same place he's been for nearly ten years, even during ill-fated marriage number two.

"I know what you're thinking. I *always* do, Larry. I should let the departed be still, but I can't. Not anymore. I will regret to *my* dying day not pursuing a lawsuit against your brothers for letting you walk away by yourself. Incorrigible. Someone should have been to blame, someone other than your stubborn self." Yoly sighs and punches in her password to Northwoods High School. A rush of adrenaline pulses through her body, feeling useful again for the first time in a long time. Retirement has a way of squelching your feeling of worth, especially when you've retired as the boss and spent years fielding questions and requests all day long.

Yoly scrolls through the years 2018 and 2019 before settling on the list she needs: 2017. "Has it really been that long, Larry? Time flies when you're retired. How come it didn't fly when I was on the job?"

Yoly clicks on Junior's given name. There's nothing official for a *Junior Cash*. His grades, she finds, were adequate, B's and C's mostly. "Considering that his mom died, and his dad was busy running a restaurant, the fact that Junior stayed on track to graduate with these grades is something he should be—should have *been*—proud of." Yoly makes the sign of the cross across her chest as she'd watched Larry do when they attended his childhood church together. "Rest in peace, Junior," she whispers. "There's a man named Larry up there who's not so good with directions but has a kind heart if you need anything."

Yoly clicks on the first folder associated with John E. Cash's name: Clubs. "Will you look at that, Larry? John sat on the bench during football and basketball, just like Arlo," she laughs. "Our boy never was any good at sports, was he? Now he's running a tech company in California and has put his mom on the bench in *his* life. Hmph! I bet Junior would have treated his mom kinder."

"What do we have here?" The microwave dings. Yoly retrieves her jasmine tea. She blows across the top and takes a slow sip. The liquid warms her soul as much as her body which gets chilled easily in a big old house. Without Larry, she'd spend hours alone in the house. She's grateful for his company, and the fact that he can't talk back isn't necessarily a bad thing. Larry had been very opinioned in life.

"I'm quite surprised to find a suspension in Junior's Discipline Folder. Hmm." Yoly reads the notation aloud.

John Cash and Wally Gordon served two after-school detentions for fighting in the cafeteria during lunch on Monday, October 4th. Mr. Grabowski witnessed the fight. John was seen pushing Wally who then retaliated with a punch to John's right cheek, dropping John to the floor. Mr. Grabowski and student Katie Thompson assisted in the breakup of the fight. Wally was interviewed by the assistant principal Heather Vincentini. He explained that he'd been eating his chicken nuggets at a table with his friends when John approached him and asked to fight. He expressed that John shoved him. He said that he punched him only in self-defense. John was also interviewed by Heather Vincentini. He said that he was walking by when Wally called him a name and blocked his path. John indicated that he pushed Wally to get out of his way when Wally then clocked him in the face. Since the fight was a he-said, he-said situation witnessed by Mr. Grabowski, a two-day suspension was warranted. It is noted that Wally was quite distraught that he'd miss the regional football game. When exiting the office, Wally spit on John, earning him a third day of suspension.

Yoly tilts her head to the side and looks at Larry's urn, as if in consideration of something important. And then it comes to her. "Aha! I was out for my hysterectomy surgery, Larry! That's why I have no memory of this fight, because I have a very good memory, don't I?"

A record of only one award sits in the Achievements Folder, a distinction for chess club participation. Yes, Junior—John E. Cash—certainly spent most of his high school career in the shadows. Using the search function on the backdoor school district site, Yoly searches for the advisor of the chess club in 2017, Hilary Painter. Yoly grits her teeth at the memory of the self-absorbed biology teacher who did not take constructive criticism well at all. She searches for Hilary's contact information and sends her an email message. There are only two things she wants to know before the Murder Movie Club meets at April's apartment on Wednesday. Did John E. Cash have any friends? Or enemies?

Chapter 9

Rishard stops at the Water's Edge Diner the next evening, not a man to delay his tasks. Rishard looks in the rearview mirror and licks his thumb to lay down a few gray strands of hair that won't stay down these days. Good enough, he decides. No one ever told him that he'd both begin to lose his hair and gain a hairstyle reminiscent of a toddler who grows hair in weird places. Rishard gets out of his car. He inhales deeply, appreciative of the view of Lake Michigan from the diner's parking lot. No matter what comes his way, the giant freshwater lake can center the soul.

The diner is quiet this late Tuesday evening. In the middle of the summer, people wait up to an hour for a seat. Rishard won't touch this place in the summer. Locals know better. There is no food in all of Northwoods that's worth an hour's wait.

A flip-flop hits Rishard in the face as he enters the diner, moving to the side to miss a mother chasing after a runaway toddler. It doesn't seem quite right to decorate the ceiling with hanging flip-flops, especially when the entrance to the restaurant can be full of patrons waiting for tables during tourist months, but he pushes away this thought. He realizes he's not only on a mission for information from Junior's dad, but he's also quite hungry.

A hostess seats him at a table in the corner of the diner with a lovely view of the lake. The sun is lowering in the sky, a beautiful patchwork of oranges and yellows streaking across the horizon. "Erin will be right with you, sir," says the hostess.

"Great. Thanks. I was wondering if John might be in today. I'm an old friend."

The hostess looks taken aback, but Rishard is confident he knows the answer to that question. Most men would not go to work the day after finding out that their only son had been murdered, but John G. Cash is not most men.

"Let me see if I can find him. It's not a normal day for John. Can I have a name to give him?" Her front tooth is missing. Poor girl.

"My name's Rishard. John will know who I am, the only Rishard in all of Northwestern Michigan, I believe."

"I don't recall John mentioning a friend named Rishard."

Rishard looks more carefully at the woman. Besides a missing front tooth, she's having a bad hair day, even worse than going bald. Her roots need a touch-up. The gray's popping out like crazy, and she could use a fresh manicure. It's the smeared makeup down her face—though it looks as if she attempted to wipe it away—that worries Rishard most. "Are you feeling alright, ma'am?"

"Me? Why? Well, I…it's been a rough day. I received some sad news last night. I lost someone very special."

"I am so sorry."

"Thank you. No one knows. I mean no one knows that *I* lost someone special, too."

"I'm sorry," Rishard repeats because he's not sure he understands the dilemma. Can't she just tell her co-workers what she's dealing with today?

"I'll get John. Thanks…thanks for listening."

"I have big ears for a reason—to listen with." Rishard laughs, "though I have four ex-wives who beg to differ with their effectiveness." Rishard wiggles his ears with his fingers, and the woman laughs before walking away a little bit lighter.

John G. Cash walks from the back kitchen area toward Rishard's table. He's wearing navy blue sweatpants and a white Northwoods High School sweatshirt that looks too small. His thinning hair makes Rishard's hair look like a crown. Rishard begins to doubt his task. He stands up from the table and extends his hand toward the bereaved father. "John, it's nice to see you again."

John tilts his head to the side to consider Rishard. "Do I know you?" he asks more gruffly than he means.

"Singles' ballroom dance class," he says, "between wives, my wives that is." Rishard laughs as John looks more closely at him.

"That was a really long time ago. Years even," says John.

"I know. I wish I could say that I've kept up on my dance moves, but I'd be lying." Rishard chuckles uncomfortably.

"Why did you ask for me?" John glances at the hostess who smiles encouragingly.

"I was hoping you'd join me for coffee."

"Coffee?"

"I'm here to help, John. Really. I want to help you. I heard about your son. I knew your son."

"You…you knew Junior?"

"I did. Good kid, well, young man."

John sits down slowly and waves over the waitress to fill the coffee mugs that are already sitting on the table. When the mugs are filled, John leans over his coffee and waits for Rishard to talk.

"I assume the police informed you of the nature of Junior's death yesterday."

"Yes. They came to the diner."

"It must have been quite a shock."

"Yes, very much so."

"While the police have a job to do, my friends and I from the movie theater have a special interest in figuring out who did this to your son."

"And what interest might that be? Were you friends of Junior? No offense, but you're older than me. You're not exactly contemporaries with my son."

Rishard smiles and nods his head. "Right you are about that. My friends and I attend a special Monday afternoon matinee every month. We've been going for months now. Junior is the first to greet us every week with his jovial personality. He makes—*made*—a killer popcorn. Uh, poor choice of words. Sorry."

"I see. Junior loved his job. It was only supposed to be temporary. I wanted him to go to college, find something of interest."

"You didn't want him to take over the diner?" Rishard asks because he's seriously curious.

John shakes his head adamantly. "No way. Restaurant work is hard work. It's life consuming. Heck, I'm here the day after I found out about my son's death. I can't miss work. Someone always needs something. Staff is always short. Bills always need to be paid."

"I imagine it's a diversion, too?"

"Yes, that. I had greater dreams for Junior. He seemed interested in the business of the movie theater. The manager kind of took him under her wing, showed him the business end of things. He had it in his mind that maybe someday he could open his own theater. But it was only a dream. He couldn't possibly make enough money *working* at a movie theater to *buy* his own theater." John lowers his chin to his chest, and Rishard worries that he might cry.

"I'm sure you were very proud of Junior."

"I was. I am. I was. Both of us were."

"Both of you?"

John looks at the hostess as she seats a young family. "I didn't stay single too much longer after those singles' ballroom lessons. Wendy and I have been together for many years."

"Ah, that makes sense. She said that she'd lost someone important."

John purses his lips together and exhales loudly. "Junior is the reason we never legally formalized our relationship. He didn't care for me moving on in my life, though it's been a long time since his mama died. They played nice in my presence at least."

"I'm sorry to hear that."

"Who'd imagine that two people would vie for my attention? That *I'd* be the source of their jealousy?" John lets out a long sigh and takes another sip of his coffee. He taps his mug a few times before snapping his head up until he is staring intently into Rishard's eyes. "Wait a second. I know what you mean about having a special interest in figuring out what happened to my son." Rishard says nothing. "You're part of that Murder Movie Club, aren't you? Don't tell me you and your silly friends are using Junior's murder as a test case for your so-called sleuthing skills. You have some nerve, Rishard." John stands up abruptly and dumps the remains of his now-cooled coffee onto the top of Rishard's head.

Rishard accepts his punishment. He knows he deserves it.

"And you were a terrible ballroom dancer."

Chapter 10

"Well, if you ask me, somebody had it out for that boy. No one just walks into a movie theater in the middle of the day on a Monday and sticks a knife through someone's chest," says Vicki as she shampoos Bernice Baker's hair in her sink.

Bernice sits up so quickly, she hits her head on the sprayer. "Ouch! What's this about a knife? I didn't hear anything about a knife! Who told you that, Vicki?"

Vicki's face turns three shades of red before she can answer. "I…well, I guess I just assumed." She raises her shoulders and turns the sprayer back onto Bernice's head before she asks any more questions. She snaps the yellow rubber band on her left wrist, a token from her daughter to remind herself to *shut her big mouth,* as Marisol likes to say when talking about her mother's penchant for gossip. She won't wear it anywhere but in the salon, though.

When Bernice is back in Vicki's chair for her weekly blowout, she starts talking about her granddaughter's beauty pageant and how much money it's going to cost her parents to participate. Vicki's mind wanders to the conversation happening at the station next to hers, a much more entertaining discussion about crime in Northwoods. "Do you really think the crime rate in Northwoods is risin'?" she asks Joanna Parks who's getting her hair colored a different color for the third time this year. This time it's green.

"Crime? I'm talking about pageants," says Bernice, very much confused by Vicki's question.

Vicki shushes her abruptly with a wave of her hand as she looks between Javier and Joanna. Javier's used to Vicki interrupting his client conversations, so he continues his work.

"Don't get me wrong. I think Northwoods is a lovely community. We're blessed with gorgeous nature, except for the rough winter if that's not your thing, but this murder in downtown has me rattled. It was the only topic of conversation at the Wine and Whine Event last night."

"What's a Wine and Whine Event?" asks Bernice, who has given up on pageant talk.

"It's pretty much just a chance to drink and complain about our problems with our besties, usually problems with men!" says Joanna. "No offense, Javier."

"None taken."

"Did you talk about drugs, by chance?" asks Vicki.

Joanna wrinkles her nose. "Drugs? No. That never came up. Why?"

"No reason. Well, okay, maybe there's a reason." She snaps the band on her wrist, but it does her no good because she keeps prying. "Do you think that drugs might have been a motive for Junior's death?"

"Hmm, well, I guess drugs is a pretty good motive for doing lots of bad things," says Joanna.

"My daughter told me that her neighbor's been growing marijuana illegally in his backyard. Do you think that has anything to do with Junior's death?" asks Bernice.

Javier laughs and rolls his eyes behind Bernice's back. Joanna smiles politely and says, "I don't think a little backyard marijuana is going to lead anyone to murder."

"Suit yourself, but Wally Gordon is big trouble. Mark my words. If he didn't murder someone, he might."

"Wally Gordon?" asks Vicki.

"That's what I said," says Bernice. "Do you know him?"

"No, but I've heard a thing or two about him in my chair. We hear a few things in the salon," says Vicki.

"Uh-huh, uh-huh, oh girls, yes we do!" Javier makes everyone laugh.

Vicki finishes beautifying Bernice to the best of her ability. Not everyone is meant to be beautiful, at least not on the outside, but Vicki does her best with what she's given. After Bernice has left, Vicki gives her own head of hair a fresh spray. All this talk of crime has made her hair fall a half inch which destresses Vicki greatly.

"Vicki, I heard you talking to Bernice when she was in the sink," says Javier. The exaggerated sleeves of his shirt smack into Vicki's face as he snaps her rubber band for her, something he's been given permission to do.

Vicki smiles coyly. "Oh, Javier, you mustn't eavesdrop. It's not nice."

"I'll ignore your teasing. But seriously, how do you know about that knife?"

"Whatever do you mean?" She clutches her chest dramatically and leans back against the counter. Javier cold stares at Vicki until she breaks. "Fine. I may have some insider information."

"From your Murder Movie Club?"

"Yes. Don't tell anyone, Javi, but we may have been there shortly after the crime."

"Vicki! How could you keep this secret from me?"

"It's a police matter. It's not my place to share the secrets of the investigation."

"Since when has something stopped you from talking?"

"Fiddle dee. If we want Northwoods to continue to be known as one of the best places to visit in Michigan, we can't be known for crime. Crime kills tourism."

"Fair. What's your theory?"

Vicki glances at the seating area where Mel Thompson is waiting for her color. "Let me ask a few more questions. I'll get back to you."

"I'd better hear that band snapping, girl."

"This isn't gossip, Javi. This is research."

"Right. Research. Got it." He laughs as he walks to the front desk to answer the phone.

Mel Thompson is a regular in Vicki's chair since she took her first client thirty-eight years ago when she was fresh out of beauty school. Mel was a classmate, having graduated with Vicki from Northwoods High School decades before Yoly became the principal. She'd been Vicki's first color job, and even though Vicki overmixed the dye, Mel came back for a second shot at it for which Vicki has been forever grateful.

"Oh, Mel! I've been lookin' forward to seein' you all day today. Can you believe the news in Northwoods?"

"Vicki, I'm so distraught. I can't stop thinking about that poor young man."

Vicki catches Javier's eyes full of judgment and merriment but continues with the ruse. "I truly can't believe that something so horrible would happen in our little town. But," Vicki pauses, "I *was* wonderin' if you've talked with your niece.

"Katie? What's Katie got to do with this?" Mel turns around to look at Vicki straight in the face.

"No, no, no. I don't think that sweet Katie had anything to do with this. All I mean is that recently you mentioned that Junior may have gotten into some trouble with Wally Gordon, you know…" she says, whispering over Mel's shoulder, "drugs."

"Oh, that. Vicki, you know me. I'm always running my mouth about something without having all the facts. Katie and Wally broke up anyway. Whatever I said about Junior taking drugs likely wasn't rooted in the good word of truth. Katie's been a bit more frank about her relationship with Wally. It seems *he's* not such a gem."

Vicki nods her head. "Yes. I heard about his backyard plants."

"Backyard plants?" asks Mel. "I don't know anything about that, but Katie said Wally wasn't such a nice guy anymore, and she tired of him. He's taking it quite hard apparently."

"Young love. It's a challenge."

"As is married-for-decades love," says Mel.

"You've got that right. Do you know what Scooter did last weekend?" Vicki combs red color through Mel's hair. "He said he'd heard my message loud and clear about needin' him to help out more. Well, his attempt was an epic fail. I'd taken out some of my sweaters for fall, and they were sittin' in a pile on the bed. For some reason unknown to man, he thought that was my dirty clothes pile, so he scooped up those sweaters and washed them! *Washed them!* Thank goodness I caught them before they got into the dryer, but I had a lot of reshapin' to do. My favorite mustard sweater is likely ruined."

"Don't you think that's for the best?" asks Mel as she turns the page of *People Magazine*. "Mustard isn't your color, Vicki."

"Perhaps so, but still."

"There's something else you might find interesting, but you can't tell a soul. My Katie would be mortified if she knew I was associating her with a murder victim in any way."

Vicki shares a look with Javier before snapping her wristband three times for good measure. Gossip is a natural high for her. "Please go on."

Mel holds up the magazine as if there are lip readers in the room and whispers. "Last Friday night, Junior picked Katie up and took her on a proper first date. He took her to Taylor's Seafood Restaurant on Ravine Road, the one with the pretty views of the lake from the bluff. Then he took her home afterward, kissed her on the cheek, and thanked her for a fun night. How sweet is that? None of that wanting to get to second base or a home run or whatever it is young people say these days. He didn't make a single inappropriate move."

"That's so sweet."

"Yeah. But then he was murdered."

Chapter 11

"I don't know what you did to that cat, Mamo." Roberta stares at what she can see of Angela. She's perched on top of the refrigerator and hiding between two bags of Sun Chips—Garden Salsa and Harvest Cheddar—because Roberta and her mother Keiko each have a favorite, though Keiko has few teeth left at 97.

"I didn't do nothing to that cat. She chewed a hole in my back pillow, though, so she's lucky she scampered out of the reach of my cane. That's what I've got to say."

"Ma! My job is to keep Angela well until Pamela gets back from her trip. I can't let anything happen no matter what you think about her."

"I don't spend time thinking about animals. I've got too much to do to concern myself with your problems."

Keiko does indeed live a vibrant life within the screen of her iPad. She follows a Danish man living in isolation near a small lake in northern Denmark, a quilter in New Zealand, a deep sea diver off the coast of Madagascar, and so many more vloggers that mean nothing to Roberta who'd rather live her life in the present of Northwoods. But Keiko stays out of Roberta's business now that she minds the business of perfect strangers. And Roberta is most grateful, for when she'd agreed to let her mother live with her when it became clear she struggled on her own, she hadn't counted on the strong genes of Mamo being stronger now than when she moved in four years ago. Sometimes Roberta's own aches and pains make her feel more like the mother than the daughter.

Roberta doesn't believe her mother. It was probably some sort of strong-worded sentence in Japanese that sent Angela climbing to the highest point in the condo. Though she tries to act tough in public, Roberta has a soft spot for four-legged creatures, more so than the two-legged sort. And ever since her dog Sumo died right before her mother moved in, she's been pining for a new pet. There's no way her mother would let her get a new pet for any permanent placement. The irony of being 75 and needing her mother's permission in her own home isn't lost on her.

She waits until words drift loudly from her mother's YouTube video before pushing a kitchen chair up to the refrigerator. Even standing atop the chair, Roberta is still too short to reach the tabby cat. She climbs back down and retrieves a large spoon. Standing on the chair again, she uses the spoon to crinkle the closest bag of Sun Chips. That sends Angela scampering off the refrigerator, first landing onto the counter and then the floor where she backs under the Lazy Susan counter.

"Come here, sweetie. I won't hurt you. Ignore that old lady. She's a crabby brute." The more time Roberta spends with her mother, the more she becomes her, but there's no self-reflection for Roberta tonight. She opens the refrigerator and retrieves a few bits of shredded cheddar cheese which she holds out for the cat. She knows that people food isn't best for cats, but she's desperate to make friends. And she doesn't want to share the chicken and rice from the crock-pot.

Angela, who hasn't eaten much since Junior fed her yesterday when he arrived at the movie theater, devours the offering. She's too hungry to still be nervous of the small lady who is holding the cheese.

As soon as Angela has eaten, Roberta scoops her up under her right arm and carries her off to her bedroom before she can protest. She shuts the door behind her, drowning out the noise from Keiko's iPad. Keiko's hearing is nearly shot, and the videos she plays carry a volume that's garnered complaints from her downstairs neighbors, at least when the windows are open. Roberta opens the bag of cat food she'd purchased yesterday and feeds Angela a proper meal. As long as the *other* little woman isn't in the same room, the cat lets down her guard.

Roberta straightens a frame on the wall as Angela eats. It holds a commendation for her service in Vietnam, *Serving the United States with distinction*, it says. She's thought about bringing it the Monthly Murder Movie Club many times, to prove to Rishard that she served proudly in Vietnam. He'd likely call it a forgery, a man threatened by a strong woman. *Typical,* she thinks. With her hand, she grazes the picture frame next to it which features a photo of a young Roberta with Keiko, her Japanese mother, and Harold, her Caucasian father. What a scandal their relationship had caused in the tiny town she'd been born into in the middle of Michigan. Roberta shakes her fist into the air, angry at no one and everyone at the same time. It's that anger that fueled her desire to join the military back in the 60s, to prove to men—men of *all* colors—that she could and should serve. She didn't see the same fighting as her male counterparts, but she was there, and she still has a tiny bullet fragment lodged in her left ankle. Her shoes aren't just for show. They provide the support she needs should that fragment ever shift and take out her balance. Nothing gives her more pride than those 18 months in Vietnam. And though hardened by her experiences and short of patience, she'd do it all again, too.

Roberta sits on the bed, waiting for Angela to finish eating. Cautiously, she walks up to Roberta's slippers and smells the stuffed Great Danes that encompass her tiny feet, a nod to Sumo. "It's okay. I'm safe. I'm a friend," she says.

Angela considers her, cocking her head to the side, before deciding to jump onto the bed. "I knew you'd come around!" Roberta strokes her brown and white fur. She thinks she hears a faint purr, though her hearing isn't what it used to be.

As Roberta pets Angela, something surprising causes her to gasp in shock. She lifts the bottom of each of Angela's four paws. And under each paw is a dark red stain. She runs her fingers over the paw pads as dry blood flakes off onto her white bedspread. "Blood," she says. "Why, Angela! You weren't outside for long, were you? Were you set free from Pamela's office *before* Junior was killed? Oh, poor Angela. Did you witness the murder?" Roberta scoops up the cat and smothers her face in her fur and sings a Japanese melody from her youth, a song her own mother used to sing to her before life made Mamo bitter. And Roberta wonders if she's turning into her mother.

Roberta tucks Angela under her silk sheets and props her head up with her pillow. Sumo took up the entire bed, of course, as Great Danes will do, but Angela looks like a spoiled princess, though a cantankerous one.

She pulls her phone from her beach bag on the floor and opens the photos app. She studies the pictures she'd snapped of the knife. Of course, she could study the actual knife as it's still in her purse, but even Roberta knows she's tampered with enough evidence for one week. The pictures are all she needs. She zooms in on the handle, the blade itself looking ordinary except for its sharpness, clearly enough to end the life of a man. Two intersecting snakes climb up the handle of the knife, both snakes with mouths opened wide and hissing tongues. It seems much too pretty to be a weapon of such violence.

"Roberta! Roberta! I need my meds! *ROBERTA!*"

"Ugh. I'm coming! Hold your horses!" Roberta places the knife on the nightstand and marches angrily into the kitchen.

"It's 4:00, Roberta. You know how I get the squirts if I don't get my probiotics."

"Mamo! Stop. I'm coming. Probiotics don't have to be given at the exact same time every day!" She shudders and wonders who is going to take care of *her* when she's 97. Gary died a month after Sumo died. She doesn't hold one death as more significant than the other. Both shattered her to her core. Their only child lives in Africa, doing good things with the Peace Corps or something like that, he says. *But what about doing good things for his mom?* Roberta wonders often. Will she be forced to live in a home? She can't accept such a fate as have so many of her friends. That's why she attends the Monthly Murder Movie Club, to keep her mind sharp. And having an enemy to tangle with in the form of a man who fancies himself attractive in Hawaiian shirts and Crocs amuses her.

    She reaches for the Tuesday afternoon pills, fills a glass with water, and places the items on the end table next to Mamo's recliner. She has paused her video on an image of a shirtless man holding up a large fish, a salmon perhaps. Roberta's not sure. "There you go. Are you happy? Anything else I can get for you while I'm here?"

    "Dinner maybe?" Mamo asks.

    Mamo's wrinkles around her mouth are so pronounced when she talks now that Roberta's amazed that there's any skin on her face at all and not just corrugated cardboard like the kind used as package filling. She doesn't feel bad at all about these cruel thoughts. Goodness knows Mamo's been finding fault in Roberta since the day she was born, and it started with her too tiny feet that caused *a nightmare when shoe shopping,* she'd heard for decades. "It's 4:00, Mamo. We go through this every night. I start dinner at 5:00. We eat at 5:30."

"And bed at 6:30. That just doesn't give me enough time to get in a movie after dinner, Roberta. Did you know you could find full-length movies on the YouTubes? For free, too! Course they're from a couple years back, like the 80s, but still…*free.*"

"The 80s were more than a couple of years ago, Mamo."

"Maybe you can start dinner at 4:30?" Mamo squeezes Roberta's hand which melts her heart in ways she didn't know were possible.

"I'll see what I can do—for tonight. Plus, most of dinner is already in the crock-pot. Don't get used to it. Now I have some work to do."

"Thank you, Robs. I'll let you know how much this fish weighs when Peter's done wrangling it in."

"Okay. Can't wait." Roberta bats her eyelashes repeatedly in annoyance as she walks away.

Angela's awake from her catnap when Roberta returns to her bedroom. In fact, she's discovered the knife—sniffing it—and one tongue's length away from ruining any chance at finding fingerprints. "Angela! No! Get out of my bag!" Roberta shoos the cat away. When she does, she notices what appears to be an inscription of some sort on the end of the knife. "Would you look at that? I guess I missed an important picture opportunity."

Roberta puts on her reading glasses to read the inscription on the end of the handle, careful not to touch it. And there, in tiny print, she finds a message of some sort.

For DD, Keep Killing It

"Well, isn't that something, Angela?" asks Roberta to the animal that has fallen blissfully asleep again on Roberta's pillow. "I wonder who DD might be. Could those be the initials of our killer?" Roberta strokes her chin and discovers new hairs she'd missed during her morning plucking. "Would he or *she* be so bold as to leave a calling card like this? I can't wait to see what the Murder Movie Club thinks tomorrow."

"Roberta! It's 4:30!" yells Mamo.

"But first, dinner." She shuts the door to keep Angela from Mamo. Not for Mamo's protection, but for Angela's.

Chapter 12

April walks with Giana around her apartment, bouncing her in her arms as she'd been taught. Nothing seems to work to settle her six-month-old baby. April looks out the window of her apartment at the brick wall of the next apartment building which looks close enough to touch, the wall she's supposed to be staring at right now over her laptop. To imagine that a year ago, April was working in a bustling marketing agency in the tallest building in Northwoods, a building with a view of Lake Michigan and a department with people—actual people to talk to—who asked her out for drinks after work or on shopping excursions. Now, since she doesn't have money for decent child care (because goodness knows her mom wasn't going to help out), April had accepted the company's solution to work from home. Grateful that she still had a job of any kind, April had been confident that life was falling into place after the shocking pregnancy announcement, but no one prepared her for a fussy baby and the torture of staring at a blank wall day in and day out. After settling Giana for her morning nap, the first thing April intends to do is create a more pleasant workspace. She's due to go crazy if she has to count the number of bricks that cross a horizontal row of the building next door one more time. Nothing holds her focus more these days than those dreary bricks.

"There you go, baby girl. Shhh, shhh, shhh. You'll feel so much better with a nap. I would *love* to take a nap. Do you know how lucky you are, Giana? You can nap any time you like. In fact, people *love* it when a baby naps. It's expected. There's no judgment at all. How lovely that would be."

After what seems like hours but is no more than fifteen minutes, baby Giana accepts her pink binky and closes her eyes, settling into a comfortable pose in her mother's arms. April allows herself to smile at her perfect baby, all fingers and toes, good health despite April's challenging, high-risk pregnancy at the age of 42. And for a brief moment, April finds peace and gratitude. She lays Giana in her crib in the one bedroom she shares with her daughter before returning to the living room. She assesses the small space, racking her brain for inspiration. "Think, April. You work in marketing. How would you market your space to look more inviting? To work more productively?"

Of course, April's no fool. The redesigning of her living space has more to do with the intrusion of the Monthly Murder Movie Club in her apartment tonight than working her day job more productively. How had she allowed Roberta to insist that *she* host the group of oddly assembled movie enthusiasts to try to solve the murder of Junior Cash? And what if Giana cries the entire time? What will they think of her then? Surely their acceptance of the single mother with no partner was just a ruse, she thinks. Even April's own mother nearly shunned her when she announced her pregnancy, though she'd bugged her for a grandchild ever since she had her first serious relationship when she was 23. Levi, the one who got away. Levi, who went to one of those smart schools out east. Levi, who became a cardiologist and had three beautiful children and a stunning wife, not that April followed his life on social media—at least not more than once a week.

All of the reminiscing and regretting about Levi reminds April that she wants to talk to Noah. She pulls her phone from her back pocket and finds his number. She still remembers the day he'd given her his number. It was right after her first interaction with Jeff the insurance salesman, in town for a conference. Back then she didn't have any attachments. And Noah didn't either. She'd first met Noah at a coffee shop 15 months ago when their coffee orders got mixed up, and they'd had a sweet laugh over the situation.

For a brief moment, she'd imagined sharing the endearing story at their wedding during the speeches portion of the reception. They'd exchanged numbers, but a week later she found out she was pregnant with Giana. She didn't have the heart to return his call when it came.

Her fingers shake as she hovers them above his name. If she doesn't have anything to contribute tonight, she will feel even lower than she does right now. "Get it together, April." She smacks herself lightly in the face, takes a deep breath, and pushes the call button.

It doesn't take long for the jovial voice of her fairy tale mate to answer. "Hello?"

"Hey." April sits on the arm of her couch and twirls her blonde hair around her fingers as if she's a shy sixteen-year-old.

"Uh, can I help you?"

"Oh, yeah. Sorry." April's heart drops as she realizes that her name didn't remain in Noah's contact list the way his had in hers. "This is April Melvin, from the movie theater. I mean, that's where I know you from. We saw each other on Monday, over Junior, uh, I mean when we—"

"Hey, April. Sorry. I didn't recognize the number. How are you today? Did you happen to catch the sunset? It was a beauty."

"I, uh, no. Sorry. I was up, of course, with the baby. But I don't have much of a view from my building. Sorry I missed it."

"I doubt you called to talk about the sun. I'm wasting your time carrying on. It's just that I haven't talked to another person today." He laughs, and April feels even more of a kindred connection than she felt when their hands first brushed against each other as they switched to-go coffees. "I've been doing a deep cleaning of the movie theater, what with it being closed down right now. Do you know how many wads of gum I've found today under seats?"

"I don't know."

"It was a rhetorical question, April, but the answer has to be near 100. Isn't that crazy? Oops, there I go again running my mouth. I'm sure you didn't call to talk about gum, either. What's up?"

April slides down the arm of the couch and clutches a pillow to her chest. Talking with Noah is so calming, like receiving a big bear hug on your lowest day. "I've been thinking a lot about what happened at the theater on

Monday. Do you remember that key I found near the candy counter?"

"I remember. Some of your friends thought it might be a theater key."

"Right. And you didn't think so. Why is that again?"

"Pamela runs a tight ship. She doesn't like people getting involved in her business. She has a lot of pride in the theater. She doesn't want people to know when she's having problems, so she wouldn't want anyone—"

"Excuse me, sorry to interrupt. What kinds of problems might Pamela be having at the theater?"

Silence passes between the two potential lovers, if only in April's mind. "April, can you keep a secret?"

"A secret? I can. I can keep a secret," though she makes no promise to keep *this secret*.

"Northwoods Theater has been experiencing some financial trouble recently."

"Really? I had no idea. Every time I pass by, the parking lot looks full."

"That's the problem. The theater *is* busy, but yet Pamela's having a hard time paying her bills. She's very distressed. I found her crying in her office one day. She's convinced herself that someone's out to bring down the theater, but she doesn't know who or why. She even involved the police, and they called Junior and me both to the station to answer questions. We didn't have anything useful to offer. Then she said she needed to clear her mind and think things through. That's why she took her vacation now, which happily coincides with a slightly less crowded Northwoods this time of year."

"Wow! I'm sorry to hear about the problems with money. I hope Pamela gets some clarity while she's away, though I imagine that Junior's death only complicates things for her. No one wants the distinction as the location of a murder on their premises."

"That's the truth. *That mess* was one area where Pamela gave me permission to bring in a special cleaning crew that handles that kind of thing. I wasn't about to touch the lobby after the police finally left."

"I don't blame you."

"You've been really helpful, Noah. Thanks for your time."

"No problem. I hope you figure out what that key goes to, but I can't imagine it belongs to the theater."

"Thanks. And I hope…I hope your girlfriend likes the jewelry you bought her. She's a lucky girl." April buries her face in a couch pillow and silently screams after the words escape her mouth.

Noah laughs. "You remember? That's really nice, April. I hope so, too. Have a great day. I need to clean spiderwebs off the curtains in front of the screen now."

"I hope you don't get a spider bite!" *Stupid, stupid, stupid,* she thinks. And before she can do any more harm to her ego, she pushes the end button on her call.

April spends the next half hour rage arranging her living room. Rage at her desperation. Rage at her life predicament. Rage at herself for raging about her life predicament. When she hears the whimpers of Giana coming from the bedroom, she's done. She looks around the room. She smiles. What a world of difference. Her desk now sits in front of the sliding door to the balcony. There's still room to walk outside, and when Giana's mobile the desk will provide an extra level of protection from dangerous exploration. A plant from the bedroom sits on the end table along with a scattering of expired home interior magazines from her mother. She'd blacked out the dates to avoid embarrassment. From the linen closet, April's pulled out a bright yellow throw blanket and draped it over the back of the couch hiding a small, spilled margarita stain. She put the two accent chairs at an angle so that a more polished seating area emerges with the simple furniture April owns. Only a few more things to do, and she won't be half as embarrassed to host the club tonight as she felt she would be this morning when she awoke and missed the sunrise entirely.

      When Giana's been fed and changed, April puts her in her car seat, the kind that attaches to a stroller. She locks her door and waits for the elevator in the hallway. April struggles into the space, using her butt to keep the doors from shutting before getting Giana and her stroller through, despite finding a man in the elevator who hasn't looked up from his phone. April swears off men again, thankful that Jeff the insurance salesman has never returned to Northwoods from Detroit even after finding out about his daughter's birth.

      April pushes the stroller along the downtown streets of Northwoods. To live in a vacation paradise isn't such a bad parental choice. The first stop April makes is to the local hardware store. On a Tuesday afternoon, the hardware store is filled mostly with men that look like contractors on missions to find what they are looking for in exactly the places where they will find them. April, on the other hand, stands surveying the store with a sweep of her eyes until a young woman asks how she might help her.

"I'd like to talk with someone about copying keys," she says, pulling back her shoulders and trying to look as if she belongs in a hardware store just as much as the men in the aisles of tools and supplies.

"I can help you. Follow me."

Giana bats at the toys that hang above her car seat, happily content with the simplicity of her life. April could stand to learn a lesson from her daughter's approach to life. The store employee leads April to a counter in the middle of the store where a man stands mixing paint in a machine that causes the items on top of the counter to vibrate. Giana's binky falls out of her mouth as her bottom lip quivers, but then the machine stops. April inserts the binky, and all is right with the world again for the moment.

"Douglas can help you."

"Thanks."

The man looks at April as the woman walks away. "Need some new paint for remodeling? The color samples are over there."

April glances at the paint samples before shaking her head. "No, I'm not remodeling. I was hoping you might be able to help me with this key." She presents the key she'd found near the counter on the day that Junior died.

 The man picks it up and turns it around. He doesn't speak as he looks from Giana to April's left hand—April's bare left hand—specifically her empty ring finger. April senses his line of thought and closes her fingers into a fist. Douglas looks up at her without a smile or a frown, straight-faced yet telling of his thoughts. "It must be very hard to find your boyfriend's mistress's key. This happens about once a week. I'm afraid I can't help you, miss."

 "What? No! I...I do not have a boyfriend."

 Douglas raises his eyebrows and smirks. "Well, either way, I can't help with that little predicament, either."

 "Hey! I'm not in a predicament, not like you think." April can caste her life circumstances as a predicament, but the minute someone *else* makes that judgment, her defenses come out, the mama bear instinct to protect her little family. April takes a deep breath. "I am here to see if you can tell me who from the Northwoods Movie Theater made this key copy. I need...I need to figure out which of the employees lost their key. The manager is out of town, and...well, someone may need the key." April bites her bottom lip, hoping that her lie will carry some truth with Douglas.

"Oh! Sure, yeah, that's an easy question to answer."

"Really?" April hopes she doesn't sound as excited as she feels.

"Junior Cash came in over a month ago to make a copy of his key. Funny young man. Made the best popcorn in town, though. He wore the original around his neck. It seemed a silly fashion choice. His girlfriend had to help him remove it when the key got stuck in his hoodie." He smiles at the memory.

"His girlfriend?"

"I don't know everything, miss, but the way they were giggly with each other, I'd have called her that. Pretty girl, long red hair. Pretty red, too—not that orange-red color like my ex-wife had.'"

"That explains a lot," April mutters under her breath.

"Excuse me?"

"Nothing. Thanks for your help." April pushes Giana's stroller out of the hardware store, happy to know that Douglas's carrot-haired wife kicked him to the curb. Even if that's not what really happened, April takes great joy in imagining it.

After a quick stop at Delish for some sweet treats for tonight's guests, April accepts the open door from a kind old woman as she pushes her stroller into the five-and-dime store. She picks up a fresh set of brightly colored throw pillows and another plant before returning home, exhausted but happy. "Who needs a man?" she asks Giana who is now wide awake and in need of a diaper change and a feeding. "We've got each other, G. We are going to be fine," she says out loud even if she's not one hundred percent convinced.

Chapter 13

Roberta is the first to arrive at April's apartment, naturally. Most in the Monthly Murder Movie Club think it's because she's afraid people will talk about her behind her back if she comes later. She's not wrong. She thrusts a package of Little Debbie pumpkins into April's hands before walking into the kitchen as if she's been here before.

"Hello, Roberta," says April. She wants to ask Roberta to take off her shoes. It *is* the polite thing to do when you're a guest in someone's home, but she doesn't want a battle. Plus, Giana's not crawling yet, so she'll just run a vacuum through the room after everyone has gone home.

"That plant needs more water, or it will die."

"Thanks. It's new."

"You have the budget to buy plants with a young child?" asks Roberta with an accusatory tone in her voice.

"It's just a plant."

"I suppose."

A knock at the door ends the awkward conversation between the two women that have little in common other than their love for murder mysteries, the ones on the screen—and now—the one in reality.

Rishard and Yoly arrive together, though only by accident. Yoly has no interest in renewing a love affair in her life. With the passing of Larry and the kick-out-the-door of Vinnie, she's quite content to spend her days alone. Alone with Larry. In his urn, that is. Plus, Rishard's already in his 60s and too set in his ways. He wouldn't mind a chance, though.

"April, your place is darling!" says Yoly, giving April a quick hug as she takes a charcuterie board full of sliced sausage and cheese into the kitchen. She sets the perfectly organized board next to Roberta's cardboard box of individually wrapped pumpkins and can't stop herself from feeling superior.

Rishard, dressed in a Hawaiian shirt with pineapples today, sheds his Crocs like a proper guest next to the door. He'd had the good sense to wear socks. He hands April a bottle of wine. "I thought we might need something to drink with all these snacks. Plus, I don't cook much."

"You could have fooled me," says Roberta, looking pointedly at Rishard's stomach. She can't help herself sometimes.

"Play nice, kids," says Yoly. "We need to act as a team tonight. There is much to share and pick apart."

"Have I got some gossip for you!" Vicki says after letting herself into April's apartment. Today she's wearing one of her wigs, something she likes to do *to keep things interesting,* she's said many times over. It's a red curly wig which looks very reminiscent of orphan Annie, but somehow it suits her skin tone. She hands a bowl to April. "Spinach dip," she says. "I forgot the bag of tortilla chips. I assume you have something suitable to use as a replacement?"

"Uh, sure." April takes the spinach dip and places it on the counter next to the cookies she'd purchased at the bakery. While everyone is oohing and aahing over Giana in her baby swing, April goes through her sparse cabinets until finding what she's been looking for, a box of Ritz crackers with one remaining sleeve. She supposes that will have to do for the spinach dip.

"Your workspace is so quaint," says Vicki, trying to be positive. "You must love being able to look outside!"

"It beats looking out this window at the next apartment building," says Rishard, pointing to the building that she'd looked at for eight hours a day for the last six months since Giana was born.

"Yep, I make do with the space I have."

"Can I take Giana out of her swing?" asks Roberta, much to April's surprise. She hadn't considered Roberta as the grandma type, though her own mother didn't really match the sweet, pinch-the-cheeks grandma type, either.

"Sure. Go ahead. She might be fussy. She's not used to being with strangers."

"Oh, scandal! This child needs to meet the world! Get around! Come here, baby girl."

No one speaks as they watch Roberta undo the swing's safety belt. She gingerly pulls Giana into her arms, careful to support the head even though the age for that constant need is past. She sits in a chair with April's new throw pillows, placing Giana in a seated position where she can still keep an eye on the world. When her binky falls out, April moves to retrieve it, but Roberta shoos her away with a flick of the wrist. "She's fine, April. No need for mouth support."

After waiting for a wail to come that never does, April sits on the couch across from her child. Not knowing what to do with herself, she sits on her hands to contain her nervous energy and looks at Yoly to pull this meeting together.

"Great! Everyone else, take a seat in April's lovely home. We have a lot of work to do." She reaches into her bag and pulls out a long cylinder box. She removes the cap from the end and takes out a scroll of paper. It's as if Santa's list of deliveries has emerged for all to see, only it's blank. Roberta had relinquished her attempt at note taking on the day of the murder. There is no stopping Yoly's drive for control in this important matter. "April, you won't mind if I tack this to the wall, will you? I couldn't find my giant pad of paper, so I had to bring this instead."

"Oh, um, well, I'm a renter. I guess a tack wouldn't be all that much different from a nail. Be sure not to use a Sharpie when you write!"

"Silly, April. I'm a school principal. I have more sense than that."

"Former principal," mutters Roberta. "I'd have found my pad of paper."

Yoly ignores her comment and proceeds to take down a painting of Lake Michigan, the most expensive piece of artwork April had ever purchased. It had come from an art show on the bluff, the same weekend she met Jeff. She doesn't need any more reminders of him anyway.

After Yoly has successfully tacked the large scroll of paper to the wall, she looks over the assembled group of what, to some, seems like a group of strangers who all showed up at the same place at the same time only because they had a train to catch or perhaps a plane. But, no, this group has come together, bound by a love for mystery, specifically murder mystery. Somehow, it works. And perhaps there's something even deeper drawing them together, a need for community, but no one's focusing on the sentimental tonight.

"Can I go first?" Vicki claps her hands together gleefully. "I have so much to say!"

"Can someone get me a drink? I have a headache already," says Roberta. Giana giggles as she stares down at Roberta's shoes as she tap dances her feet, much to the baby's joy.

Rather than argue, Rishard fills a glass half full with wine and deposits it on the end table nearest Roberta. Even he knows when to be nice.

"Yes, Vicki. You may go first." Yoly write's *The Murder of Junior Cash* across the top of the paper scroll in neon green marker, the Crayola kind that would be on every school child's class list of supplies. April grins, a callback to her youth that makes her happy. She loved school, and she hopes that Yoly has a pastel pack of markers with her, too.

Vicki stands up likes she's going to accept an award as best beautician in all of Northern Michigan. She tightens the red scarf around her neck and gives a nod to each of the people before her as she begins her presentation. "I am honored to be here tonight to share my gossip, uh, the news I've learned about our case. I think you will find what I have to say quite interesting." She pauses for dramatic effect, but only Giana reacts, with the cutest baby toot heard to man, sending everyone into a fit of laughter except for Roberta who holds the baby out as if she were contagious. She hands her back to April. April changes the baby on a mat she puts on the floor in the hallway as she doesn't want to miss any of the gossip Vicki has to share.

"Yoly, how would you like to categorize the information we share tonight?" Vicki asks.

"I guess I'm going to wait to hear what you have to say to see if a natural organization shows up. How does that sound?"

Everyone nods in agreement. Rishard grabs a bowl from April's cabinet without asking and fills it with two spoonfuls of spinach dip and a quarter of the remaining Ritz crackers.

"I need to maintain the privacy of my sources," says Vicki as Rishard deposits himself on the middle of the couch.

"Of course."

"Yes, yes."

"Go on."

"Junior had a date on Friday night!" She clutches her chest and beams. "And he was a true gentleman. He maintained complete decorum throughout the entire night."

"What's that got to do with murder?" asks Roberta. "Lots of people go on dates, well, not everyone. "Some people just hook up. To each their own." She looks away as April re-enters the room with a sleeping Giana in her arms. April wishes she could evaporate or click a pair of mythical shoes and disappear, maybe something like the shoes on Roberta's feet. Instead, she straightens her shoulders and walks into the room as if she owns it because she does. Well, at least, she rents it. No one's allowed to insult her in her own home.

Disgusted by Roberta's outrageous statement, Yoly takes control of the situation. "Let's try to stay on topic, shall we? We are a team here, the Monthly Murder Movie Club.

We have the same motives and intentions. Let's focus on Junior. Thank you for sharing. I'll add a category heading that says, *Junior's Behavior and Traits*. I'll add *date* underneath. Vicki, do you have any more information regarding this date?"

"I do! He went on a date with Katie Thompson!"

"Is that supposed to mean anything that he went on a date with this young lady?" asks Rishard. He has a bit of spinach on his chin, but no one tells him.

"From my sources—my most *reputable sources*—Katie had recently ended a relationship with Wally Gordon."

"Is that the young man you mentioned might have been involved in drugs with Junior?" asks April.

"Good memory! Excellent listening skills, April." Vicki glares at Roberta who has lowered her eyes.

Roberta uses the attention to reach into her bag and pull out a hat, this time a simple ball cap that reads, *VETERAN*. She places it on her head, and Rishard can't stop himself. "Seriously?"

"It's my thinking hat. Shut your trap!"

"Focus!" yells Yoly, startling Giana who lets out a whimper before April gives her a binky from the coffee table.

Roberta opens her mouth like she's going to say something regrettable, but Yoly snaps her fingers at her, and she closes her mouth. "Do you have any more information about the drugs, Vicki?"

"I cannot confirm that rumor. My source was unsure. But Wally Gordon was growing marijuana plants in his backyard."

"Smart kid," says Roberta.

"Okay, I'll add another category," says Yoly. *"Peripheral Characters."* She adds Wally Gordon's name underneath.

"Thank you. That is all I have to contribute at this time." Vicki curtsies before walking to the kitchen and pouring herself a large glass of wine.

"I think this might be a good time to take a break," says Yoly. "Everyone fuel up. We have a long night ahead of us."

Chapter 14

"May I give the baby thing a go?" asks Rishard as the clubbers return to the living room. "I've only got one son and two grandsons, but I think I can handle a little girl. They're sure a lot sweeter." He smiles, and April wishes that her own dad were still alive. He'd have been a great grandpa and maybe even elevated her mother's ability to care for Giana.

"Sure, Rishard. You can take her. But if she gets fussy, I'll need to feed her. It's getting close to her bedtime."

"I understand. I can help with the feeding, too, if you'd like. Clearly, I can handle anything related to food." He pats his belly and smiles.

"You aren't breastfeeding?" asks Roberta.

If only Roberta had the ability of perspective, she might understand how much like her own mother she's become. And that knowledge would crush her if she could process it.

"Leave her be, Roberta! April, why don't you go next? What did you find out?" asks Vicki, patting a spot on the couch for April to sit down.

All eyes turn to the new mom. She wears new jeans, a treat she'd given herself a few weeks ago, mostly because none of last year's fall jeans fit, but also because she wanted something new, something other than the yoga pants and loose tops she wore working from home. "I know who made the copy of the key to the movie theater," she says quietly.

"You do?"

"What?"

"Who?"

"How?"

April smiles at their reactions, feeling useful for the first time in a very long time. "Junior made a copy of his key at the hardware store a month ago."

"Wow!" everyone says in unison.

"That's quite unusual considering Pamela was allegedly particular about keeping those keys accounted for," says Rishard.

"And his girlfriend was with him," adds April.

"Girlfriend? Katie?" asks Yoly.

"I'm not sure of her name. The employee said she had long red hair."

Vicki gasps aloud, waking Giana for a brief moment before she falls back to sleep in Rishard's arms. "That must have been Katie. She has the same beautiful hair color as her Aunt Mel though Mel needs a boost. That's why I'm so useful in town," she smiles. "But that doesn't make sense to me. According to Mel, Wally and Katie had only recently broken up. And you say that the employee at the hardware store said that the key copy was made a month ago?"

"That's what he said," says April.

"Interesting," says Vicki. She takes another sip of her wine.

"What are you thinking, Vicki?" whispers Rishard so as not to wake Giana.

"I'm not sure, but you'd better add Katie Thompson under *Peripheral Characters*. And if anyone ever tells Mel, I'll deny it up and down a thousand times."

"Sounds like that young girl made the rounds," says Roberta. She crosses her legs and kicks Rishard in the process.

"You don't know that for sure," says April, feeling a need to protect Katie's reputation though she doesn't know her at all.

"Write it down, Yoly."

"Got it. Anything else, April? That was very helpful information."

"One other thing though it might not mean anything. I spoke with Noah again." She ignores the raised eyebrows on everyone in the room. "He said that Pamela had been sad. He'd seen her crying. She'd been experiencing some sort of financial problems with the theater and didn't understand why as business seemed good, aside from some unexpected repairs. She even called the police, and they questioned Noah and Junior."

Vicki snaps her fingers. She doesn't wear her rubber band outside of the salon and has been quite excited to gossip without consequences tonight. "I bet that's why the police said they talked to him at the station and upset Junior when they called him by his given name. He hated being called John E. Cash."

"You can't blame the kid," says Rishard.

"You cannot," says Vicki. "The police must have thought that Junior had somethin' to do with Pamela's money problems with the theater."

"Not necessarily," says April. "Noah said he was questioned, too."

"And we know that sweet man doesn't do anything unethical," says Vicki. "Right, April?"

"I wouldn't know…I don't—"

"Leave April alone. She's got enough going on trying to keep it together for her daughter. She doesn't need a man interfering." Roberta looks at Giana, and April feels a simmering fire rise to the part of her brain that activates her mouth.

"I've had enough of your opinions, Roberta!" April stands up and brushes imaginary crumbs from her new jeans. "You are judgmental and rude. I think I'm doing a dang good job with my daughter, for what it's worth. And if you want to stay here for the rest of our analysis of Junior Cash's murder, then you need to stick a sock in it!"

Roberta looks surprised but indifferent. She rolls her eyes and looks away from everyone. She grunts her disapproval at being dressed down by the youngest person in the room but doesn't say a word.

"Thank you for your information, April. Well done. I'll add Pamela and Noah to the list, just because they've come up in conversation. I'll go next," says Yoly. "I checked my records of former students." Yoly leaves out the part about accessing the records electronically due to a security lapse by Northwoods High School's Tech Department. "He was an average student, not very athletic, and thrived in the chess club."

"Ah, the more I hear about that young man, the more I like him. He really was just a nerd who had a thing for redheads and liked to blend in rather than stand out. I can relate," says Rishard.

No one believes for one moment that Rishard Logan has ever blended in. Just like with his colorful shirts and Crocs, his bright personality holds the attention of others when he walks into a room, nothing at all like Junior Cash. Still, it's sweet that he considers himself a wallflower.

"Right, Rishard. Thanks." Yoly takes a deep breath. "I also emailed his former chess club advisor Hilary Painter.

"That woman?" scoffs Roberta. She blows air aggressively through her closed lips which sounds very reminiscent of a snorting horse.

"A former run-in with this Hilary?" asks Rishard. He stands up to rock with Giana who has become irritable. Feeding time is near.

"When I volunteered at the high school—"

"You were a *volunteer?*" asks Vicki.

"She was," says Yoly, shrugging her shoulders.

"As I was saying, when I was a volunteer, Mrs. Painter sent me only the most difficult students to work with. When the students were reviewing for a biology test, do you know how inappropriate some of those boys were, pointing to things in their textbooks that were taken completely out of context? It was disgusting. And she thought it was funny. She did not care one bit when I took the matter to Yoly."

"It's true. Mrs. Painter did not like constructive criticism. Anyhow, getting back to the matter at hand, Mrs. Painter recalled the memory of a very unhealthy relationship between Wally Gordon and Junior Cash. It seems Wally bullied Junior in ways that never reached my desk. I surely would have done something about it. But that was seven years ago. I can't fix it now."

"Especially since he's dead," says Vicki.

"Yes, there's that."

"Well, he's already on your list," says Roberta. "I suppose it's just more reason to consider his whereabouts on Monday afternoon. Too bad we can't add Mrs. Painter to the list."

Yoly assesses the list before the club. "I'm not sure what to make of our list, but we still have to hear from Rishard and Roberta. Shall we regroup tomorrow night? We've already been here for an hour." Yoly looks at her watch.

"Oh no! I mean, uh, we can finish. Let's wrap this up tonight. Okay? I'll give Giana her bottle and get her ready for bed. Please continue." April has no intention of adding a second night of hosting. She's exhausted beyond belief, but she'd rather spread her exhaustion a couple more hours into one night than two. If she were being completely honest with herself, she'd admit she does like the adult contact with people she's not related to. She's missed it. They all have.

Chapter 15

With Giana down for the night, at least until everyone has gone home for the evening, April fills her plate for the first time. She looks at the assorted characters in her living room, talking animatedly. About what? It doesn't really matter. It's not the life she'd thought she'd be living a year ago. A year ago, she was making suitable strides at work, doing the dating apps thing a couple of times a month, accepting that her life wasn't taking the path of her former sorority sisters. She didn't have 2.5 kids, a wealthy husband, or a promising corporate climb in her own right. She wasn't a teacher or a lawyer. But she was content, if not lonely. She certainly didn't expect to have children. She thought that ship had sailed. No steady relationship prospects and already the occasional skipped period as perimenopause had kicked in. But here she was, a single mother with a baby, no dating prospects, a job that had taken a step backwards due to childcare demands, and an odd assortment of peers much older than herself frolicking in her living room. April smiles, though, because—for a moment—she feels happy. And that's not an emotion that's come easily in the last year.

Yoly claps her hands rhythmically, which catches the attention of her students, for that's what she thinks of them.

With ever the teacher mentality, she organizes the Monthly Murder Movie Club for round two. "Let's wrap up our personal research so that we can dig down on our theories."

"Rishard, can you please share anything that you learned from Junior's father?"

"Absolutely." Rishard stands next to Yoly. In his past life, before being forced into retirement by youthful salesmen who worked their fancy devices for boat sales far superior to Rishard's old-fashioned Rolodex contact list, he'd been able to hold his customers' attention for long periods of time. No one knew the specs of the boats on his lot like Rishard. But a combination of the economy dipping and many lot sales turning to online sales, he left his job, promising himself to spend his retirement on early morning fishing boats or late afternoon speedboat rides. But lately, he'd be lucky to rise by 9:00 and complete his three crossword puzzles' goal by dinner. The Movie Murder Club was the sole reason for the new pep in the step of his Crocs, even if he had to share his time with shoe-sparking Roberta Kato.

"As you all know, Junior's father owns and manages Water's Edge Diner," says Rishard.

"What a fantastic view they have!" says Vicki.

"It's true. They have a prime piece of property."

"Did you find Junior's dad at work? He'd just lost his son," says April, imagining for the first time what it might feel like to lose a child, and she winces.

"He was indeed at work, which I assumed. I'd taken a singles' ballroom dance class many years ago with John. Let's just say, he commits to his work, whether it's running a diner or mastering a tango or a waltz." Rishard laughs at the memory he's untucked. So does Roberta but for different reasons. Yoly shushes her. "I'll be brief as I don't have much to contribute, I'm afraid. The hostess and John have been in a longtime relationship. Her name is Wendy. Junior didn't approve, so they never married. Recall that his own mother died when he was in middle school. He did share that Junior had dreams of owning his own movie theater someday. Pamela had taken him under her wing, showed him the business end of things."

"Which is interesting as the police had to have *some* reason to call Junior in for questioning about money problems the theater was having," says Vicki.

"And Noah," April says quietly.

"Pamela clearly asked the police to talk to them both. It's obvious. There's no one else who'd make a request like that," says Roberta.

"I agree," says Rishard. "I think Pamela asked the police to speak with Junior and Noah, too, but just to satisfy her conscience that she'd considered all possibilities for the theater's financial woes, not because she believed that either man had anything to do with those problems."

"Perhaps," says Roberta.

"That's all I've got. He kicked me out."

"He kicked you out of the diner?" Vicki grabs her head in surprise, tilting her wig slightly to the right side but enough for everyone to notice.

"He figured out the club's motive for wanting to solve this murder."

"Do we have a motive?" asks April.

"Sure we do. We've been watching murder mystery movies for months now: gathering clues, finding suspects, identifying red herrings. Now's our chance to solve a *real* murder," says Rishard.

"And to do it before those incompetent police," says Roberta.

"We're helping poor Junior's family," says Yoly.

"And soon, John G. Cash will be *asking* Rishard to come back to the diner—all of us, actually—and celebrating us for figuring out who murdered his son!" says Vicki.

"But does anyone else think that we're kind of making a game out of someone else's misfortune?" April's question causes a silent pause before everyone begins to speak at the same time.

"*Somebody* has to solve this murder."

"We can't have criminals running loose."

"We're doing good for society."

"Better us than Officer Cleary. He's rude."

After Roberta's proclamation, April seems satisfied with their views. She nods her head silently, and Yoly continues. "Thank you, Rishard, for your contribution. The information about Junior's dislike of a potential stepmother puts the hostess on the list under the *Peripheral Characters* heading. I'll add his aspiration for owning a theater under *Junior*. How sad that he couldn't attain his dream." Yoly switches to a purple marker. "That leaves only Roberta."

At the mention of her name, Roberta springs up from her chair like a trick pony jumping over a barrel. "It's about dang time! I'm about to fall asleep with all of this boring information. I have some *real* clues to offer!"

"Well, get on with it then, woman. We're not spring chickens anymore!" Rishard holds his arms across his chest.

"Angela had bloody paws!" As she speaks, she jumps up and down, setting off the light show beneath her feet.

"Bloody paws? I thought she'd come from outside," says April.

"She did," says Yoly, filling in the blanks. "But someone must have let her out of Pamela's office—"

"but not Junior. He knew better than to release that angry beast," says Vicki.

"Correct," continues Yoly. "which means that someone went into Pamela's office."

"And Angela escaped," says April.

"Which means that whoever went into the office—"

"Murdered Junior," finishes April, Roberta, Rishard, and Vicki.

"There's something important in that office," says Roberta.

"And we have a key." April speaks her words so quietly she has to repeat them. "We have a key."

"Then let's go," says Roberta. "Why are we wasting time yapping here?"

Yoly adds a new category to her scroll before taking it down and stuffing it back in the cylinder.

Within minutes, the group has assembled at the door to April's apartment, all except for April. "I can't go," she says. "I have Giana."

"Don't you have one of those baby carriers that you can wear on your body?" asks Vicki.

Roberta scowls at Vicki for suggesting such a thing. "No. April's doing the right thing. I'll text you. I promise." Roberta squeezes April's hand, and a charge of gratitude passes between the two women. April gives Roberta the key with a hint of sadness.

Peripheral Characters
Wally
Katie
Pamela
Noah
Hostess/Wendy/John Cash's love interest

Junior
Date with Katie
Possible drugs

Average student
Not very athletic
Suspended after a fight with Wally

Other
Angela's bloody paws
Pamela's office opened by the killer

Chapter 16

They take Rishard's van to downtown Northwoods. There's no need to attract more attention with four vehicles arriving together at a business that's closed. With the close proximity of Northwoods Movie Theater to LC's Bar, there will be other cars on the street, though Rishard's yellow 1965 Volkswagen Bus always stands out. It's loud, both in color and sound, mostly because Rishard likes to honk the horn that sounds like *arugula, arugula* every time it's activated.

Roberta takes extra effort to climb out of the passenger seat but refuses any assistance. She's stubborn like that. Vicki and Yoly exit the van more quickly, grateful to have arrived safely as they'd had to sit in folding chairs as Rishard had removed his seats to carry a kayak to his buddy's house last weekend. Every time the van turned directions, the women would hold onto the windows to keep from toppling over, though Rishard drove under the speed limit. There are many crimes being broken by the Monthly Murder Movie Club tonight.

Vicki puts a scarf over her wig and ties it at her chin, her best effort at going incognito, though it only makes her look even more recognizable as no one in town has larger hair than Vicki. Yoly hugs her arms against her sweater to ward off the chilly, windy evening air, though at 55 degrees, this temperature would feel balmy if it were the middle of January. It's funny how that works, the same temperature feeling so very different depending upon the time of year. Rishard doesn't seem bothered, his trusty Crocs leading the group confidently toward the alley where Noah had entered with Angela on Monday. Roberta yells out, "All clear!" much too loudly but with authority before turning the key in the door that will lead them directly into the theater. She'd refused to give that responsibility over to anyone else.

Yoly shivers when they're safely inside. "It's kind of freaky being in here at night," she says. "Everything's so dark."

"A movie theater's always dark, Yoly." No one can argue with Roberta's observation, not even Rishard.

"Don't turn any lights on," says Vicki. "Use your phones."

As she pops out her own phone, it begins to ring. "Oh my lands! Oh my lands!"

"For scandal's sake, answer it!" says Roberta.

Vicki whispers as she answers. "Hello?"

"Hi, Vicki. It's April."

"April!"

"Ah, April!"

"We miss you, April!"

Roberta presses her mouth together into what can be presumed to be a slight hint of a smile.

"Sorry. I...I really wish I could be there with you all. Do you think you could carry me around, I mean carry the phone around? And tell me what's happening?"

"Sure, darlin'. I'd be honored. Thanks for choosin' *me* for this most important job." Vicki winks at Yoly who smiles. "Right now we are walkin' down the aisle of the theater. Yoly and I think it's kind of creepy."

"Tell her that the building's making creaking sounds with that wind out there," says Rishard.

"Give me that!" Roberta reaches for Vicki's phone and pushes the video camera button on the bottom of the screen. "Now you're on FaceTime. Geesh. And to think I'm the most technologically advanced in this group of misfits tonight!" She stomps ahead of everyone, her path lit only by her shoes, but her heart warm with a feeling she's not used to, despite her hard exterior. Roberta's having *fun*.

"We're enterin' the lobby now, April. The marquise sign is still lit from the building—"

"Advertising movies that no one's seeing," says Yoly.

"Say, does anyone know when Pamela's due back from her vacation? She might not take kindly to us going through her office," says Rishard.

"Do you honestly think she's going to come to her office at 10:30 on a Wednesday night? *Alone?*" asks Roberta.

"When there's been a dead body in the lobby," says April from her bedroom. She's wearing matching pajamas with sloths on them. Everyone can hear the white noise machine in the background meant to soothe Giana and provide a buffer for any noise that April is making as she talks. But no one says anything about the static noise. They're just grateful not to have to share a space with a baby anymore, even a sweet baby like Giana. Those days are distant memories for the members of the Murder Movie Club.

"Yes, good point," says Rishard.

Pamela's office door is closed but unlocked, something the club members had not considered although Roberta could pick a lock if needed. Nobody knows that, but they haven't asked. She can do a lot of things that nobody knows about.

"I can't see anything. What's going on?" asks April.

Yoly turns on a light, causing audible gasps. "What's the big deal? It's an inside office. No one can tell that we are here."

"Oh, yeah, she's right," says Vicki. She unties her scarf and stuffs it into her pocket. "What are we looking for?"

"I don't know," says Yoly. "But try not to make it look obvious that we were here."

"Why? Either Pamela is an unorganized person, or the police have already looked through her things because this room is a mess," says Rishard who has dropped to his knees and is looking through the trash can.

Everyone stakes claim on a different part of the office, looking for clues as to the murder of Junior Cash, if any such things exist. Roberta feels around the desk like a ninja, expecting something to pop open upon the touch of her hand. Vicki looks through papers on Pamela's desk, stopping to show April anything she finds interesting. Yoly scrolls through the desktop computer which is easy to get into as Pamela's password is taped to the screen, and Rishard continues to fiddle with the scraps in the trash can.

Roberta swears when she hits her head on a desk drawer that Vicki has pulled open. But after she's done spouting off, she marvels at what has landed on the floor in front of her: a key, another key.

Chapter 17

"I've found it!" yells Rishard.

"I've got it!" yells Roberta.

"What do you have?" they ask each other at the same time.

Rishard holds up a piece of paper. Roberta holds up her key.

"One at a time," says Yoly.

"What's the paper say?" asks Vicki.

"It's a notice for collections. The theater had a new roof put on five months ago."

"I remember. They were pounding so hard we missed the killer reveal during *Midwinter Murders*." Roberta sighs loudly and shakes her head, along with Rishard who also remembers because he'd been the only one to guess the correct killer that day.

"Why do you think she threw it away?" asks Vicki.

"She's probably embarrassed that she can't pay the bill, though we don't know why," says Yoly.

"Well, embarrassment isn't going to solve your money problems." Roberta takes the paper from Rishard's hand and puts it on the desk. "Let's figure out where this key goes. It was taped under the desk drawer."

"It's a safe key," says Yoly. We had a key like that at the high school where we locked up any medications the students would need to take during the day."

"You had to administer meds?" asks Vicki.

"We didn't have a nurse, so it fell to the secretary or me to hand out medication."

"Boy, you have to do a little bit of a lot of things as a school employee," says Rishard.

"More like a lot bit of a lot of things, but that's another conversation."

"Stop your blabbering and look for that safe. Mamo's gonna be furious that I'm not there to put her to bed."

"You have to put your mother to bed?" asks Rishard, generally confused because he hadn't spent much time asking Roberta about her personal life. She just scowls at him.

Meanwhile, Vicki—and April, via her phone—begins to search the room, running her hands over the tops and bottoms of chairs and checking the file cabinets. "Vicki, check that picture behind the desk!" says April, who's sitting upright, pointing to the wall behind Vicki.

"You're right! Like in *The Killer Beas*!"

"The safe behind the picture!" Yoly snaps her fingers. "Bea number 3 hid the murder weapon there!"

Rishard removes a painting of Northwoods Movie Theater that had been commissioned by the city council. They'd hired local artists to created artwork of some of the iconic businesses in Northwoods. Imbedded behind the painting is a safe that's become flush with the wall.

April claps to herself below the view of the camera. She's quite pleased to have been able to contribute to the investigation from afar but doesn't want her new friends to know how much of a natural high she's feeling at this moment, a sense of purpose outside of motherhood that she'd been missing for so long.

Yoly, Vicki, and Roberta gather around Rishard as he sets the painting on the ground. They marvel at the sleek safe that blends so well into the gray painted walls of the office. "Hand me the key, Roberta."

"Uh-uh. I've got this." She brushes against Rishard and inserts the small key into the safe, turning it before he can protest.

"What is it, Vicki? What's in the safe?" April can't contain her giddiness.

Vicki cranes her head over Yoly's shoulder as Yoly gets a mouthful of her wig. "Vicki! Step back!" Yoly spits out a synthetic piece of hair.

All of the commotion allows Roberta to reach into the safe without challenge. "It's…it's empty," she says.

"What?"

"Are you sure?"

"Oh no!"

"Let me see!" Rishard shines the light from his phone into the safe. He runs his hands along the smooth velvet at the bottom. He's about to concede that Roberta's assessment is correct when his hand touches paper near the very back of the safe. "Yoly, hold my phone and shine it in the safe, please." He hands off his phone and reaches his hand back to the paper. Half-covered by the velvet base, he pulls the half sheet of paper out from under the safe lining. "Bingo!" He snaps his fingers.

"What is it?"

"What's it say?"

"Give me that!" Roberta rips the paper from Rishard's hand while he's reveling as the hero of the night.

"Hey!" he yells.

Roberta climbs atop the desk. She's quite flexible for a woman of her age. No one will challenge her there. She waits until her audience has stopped grumbling before pulling a pair of reading glasses from her pocket. She begins to read silently which only irritates her cohorts more. No one says a word, though. They must play Roberta's game to gain any information.

"It's a certificate of authenticity," she says.

"For what?" asks Vicki.

"Let me see. I didn't get that far."

"There's a picture on the back," says Yoly, the tallest in the group and the closest to Roberta. She shines her light at the image before Roberta flips it over.

"Oh, scandal! Oh, scandal! Oh, scandal."

"Roberta! Be careful! You're going to fall!" Roberta trips over a pen holder and steps on a stapler before turning sideways.

Rishard throws out his arms. Everyone backs up as he adeptly catches Roberta as she tumbles off the desk. She looks into the eyes of her savior and scoffs. "Put me down this minute."

"You're welcome," mumbles Rishard. He sets Roberta upright again.

She clears her throat. "It's a certificate of authenticity—"

"You said that already," says April.

"I did. Let me finish. It's a certificate for the validity of a movie prop."

"What kind of movie prop?" asks Vicki. "I can't stand the suspense. Spit it out, woman!"

"For the knife used in the filming of the new Dane Dimoli movie."

"*Murder Meets Michigan*?" asks Yoly.

"Yes."

"That's pretty cool," says Rishard. "I wonder if Pamela had some sort of movie memorabilia collection."

"It's possible," says Yoly.

"And the safe *is* empty, except for the paper that looked hidden," says Rishard.

"Providing a possible motive for murder."

"Of Pamela, maybe," says Rishard, "but I don't know what Junior Cash has to do with anything in this safe."

"Junior had a great deal to do with what was in this safe," says Roberta. She hands the paper to Vicki because she stands closest. Then she scrolls through her phone before landing on the item she was searching for. "Got it!" She holds up a picture of an ornate knife handle from her photo collection.

"I don't understand, Roberta," says Vicki. "It's a very elaborate knife. I'll give you that. But is that the knife that matches the certificate from the safe? And, if so, why do *you* have a picture of it?"

Roberta swipes to the next picture, a full picture of the knife from handle to tip, the shaft still covered in blood. "Because it's the knife that was used to kill Junior Cash."

Chapter 18

After the shock has worn off, the Monthly Murder Movie Club begins to theorize and plan their next steps. "Let's move to the theater," says Yoly. "It's where we do our best thinking."

"That's an excellent idea," says Vicki. She leads the way with April by her side and lighting her path.

No one turns on the overhead lights, but the twinkling lights on the ceiling are illuminated. "Do you think those lights are always on?" asks April as Vicki turns the phone upwards for her to see the constellations as they'd be right now in the Northwoods, Michigan sky though hidden tonight by cloud cover.

"It's a marvelous thing to have those lights, quite a brilliant design," says Rishard. "My favorite time of the year is when you can see the Virgo and Sagittarius constellations at the same time."

"During the Northen Michigan Extravaganza Festival," adds Roberta. "A superb time to attend a movie in Northwoods."

For the first time today, Rishard finds himself agreeing with Roberta, until she takes her seat and pulls out her military dress hat—her thinking hat—she'd said many times. Rishard sighs, and sits down behind her, waiting for Yoly to begin the discussion into the matters that have transpired tonight.

Yoly unwinds the scroll she'd brought from April's house, "just in case" she'd explained. Now she holds up one end while Roberta holds the other from her chair. Roberta's feet don't even hit the floor, so the light from her shoes are of no help right now, which is ironic as they could use the illumination. Instead, Vicki shines her light on the paper.

"What do we know?" asks Yoly. Falling back into muscle memory from her teaching days before becoming a principal, she questions the students—of sorts—before her, the students of detective work.

"We know that Junior, John E. Cash, was killed here on Monday late mornin' or early afternoon by being stabbed in the heart with an ornate knife that we now know was the actual knife used in the filmin' of the Dane Dimoli movie we were supposed to watch on that fateful day," says Vicki, shaking her head sadly.

"*For DD. Keep killing it,*" says Roberta.

"Excuse me?"

"What was that?"

"Where'd *that* come from?"

"Oh!" Roberta holds her hand to her chest dramatically. "Did I forget to mention that the knife was engraved? Silly me."

"I'm not sure if that changes anything other than to lend more credibility to the fact that the knife was actually of value as a movie prop," says Yoly.

"It's a heck of a prop as it could *actually* kill a man," says April.

"Indeed," says Rishard. "Odd."

"Move on, people. My mother is going to be spitting fire by the time I get home. It's nearly midnight." Roberta kicks her legs in frustration which does nothing to speed up the conversation as the others silently judge the most cantankerous woman in the room having to tend to someone even worse in temperament.

"Back to what we know." Yoly redirects the conversation as best she can. "Junior loved his job. He cared about what he was doing and had dreams of opening his own theater one day. The theater had recently had some work done that lead to bills, the roof and such. Pamela, by all accounts, thought that the theater was doing well financially. However, the *actual* money didn't seem to materialize when it came to paying bills, which caused great anxiety."

"And led her to call the police who talked to Noah and Junior," says Rishard.

"But they didn't implicate them in any crime," April reminds them, feeling her face warm at the mention of Noah.

"Do you think that Pamela really came back early from vacation and killed Junior?" asks Vicki.

"Don't be silly," says Roberta. "Remember the cat? Someone let Angela out of that office. There's no way Pamela would subject her baby to a dead body, not to mention let Angela free when she left the building. We can confidently rule out Pamela's involvement."

"She's right," says Yoly, crossing off Pamela's name from the list of Peripheral Characters.

"And the police had nothing on Noah. Cross him off, too," says April.

A knowing look passes between the club members gathered together in the theater, the wanting heart of young love, even though April wouldn't consider herself young anymore. "For now, as we have nothing ominous on Noah, we can knock him off the list." Yoly crosses out his name leaving Wally Gordon, Katie Thompson, and Wendy, Junior's never-to-be stepmother.

"Cross off Wendy. She'd been with John for seven years. If Junior couldn't do anything to scare her away from being in a relationship with a man who would never marry again in deference to his son's feelings, then she wasn't going to do anything to change Junior's existence in their life. Wendy cares for *both* Johns. It was clear in the diner." Rishard hangs his head, recalling his conversation with the senior John and regretting bringing him more grief.

"That leaves Katie and Wally as persons of interest," says Yoly.

"No way Katie should be considered. She's a sweet girl. And remember how April said that the hardware store employee talked about how giggly she and Junior were in the store together. Aunt Mel told me how happy Katie had been after their date," says Vicki.

"We can all accept that Wally was a bully to Junior in his younger years, but what information do we have that he'd still tormented him as a young man?" asks Yoly.

"We need to talk to Katie," says Vicki. "Mel's always up late watchin' YouTube videos. I'll have Katie's contact information in a few minutes. If Katie confirms that Wally was still tormentin' Junior as an adult, then I think he might be our man."

"I need to call Mamo. I'll be right back." Roberta takes her phone and walks out to the lobby.

"Are you still with us, April?" asks Rishard.

"I'm here!" April waves at the camera. "Thanks for bringing me along. I imagine it's chilly in there."

"You know, surprisingly, it's rather warm," says Yoly who has removed her sweatshirt and now wears a University of Michigan T-shirt.

"Junior was probably in charge of the heat while Pamela was gone," says Rishard.

"Don't you think that the heat would have been on a timer?" asks Yoly.

"That's quite odd. Hmm." Rishard guides himself along the row of theater seats and to the front of the theater where the thermostat hangs on the wall. "Hey, guys! Guess what? The heat's on 75—"

"Well, that explains a lot," says Yoly. "I thought I was going through menopause again." She fans herself with her hands. "Turn it down!"

"There's more! There's another box here, too. Looks like part of the security system. And there's a wire in the back that's been cut."

"I didn't even consider that the theater would have a security system when we entered. Officer Cleary would be quite sour to be alerted to the presence of the Murder Movie Club back at the scene of the crime," says Vicki.

"We'd look very guilty," says April.

"The killer must have cut the security system. But, why?" Vicki taps her chin as the lights in the theater switch on, dimming the view of the constellations on the ceiling.

"What on earth?" Vicki, Yoly, and Rishard rub their eyes for clarity as they adjust to the drastic change.

An eerie clapping grows closer to the friends as a figure walks toward them. Stopping at Vicki and Yoly's row, his unexpected appearance causes the two women take a step back. Vicki lowers the phone as April goes quiet. Rishard considers running up the aisle and pounding the man in the chest as he might have done in his younger days, but he holds a large metal bat, the kind of weapon used by Edgar Beaverton in *The Baseball Massacre* that they'd watched a couple of months ago.

"Congratulations. The Monday Movie Club has it all figured out, don't they?" he asks.

"Monthly Murder Movie Club," Vicki corrects him. She can't help herself. If this is going to be the last moment that the club spends together, they at least want to go out named correctly by the murderer.

"My apologies, ma'am. The *Monthly Murder Movie Club* has lived up to its reputation, solved another murder in Northwoods, this time in real life and not on the screen. I read the little write-up about you in the Nothwoods Gazette. I even considered joining you for a matinee, so I could intimidate my little friend while he made you all popcorn. I hear he was quite a chef when it came to making popcorn. Must have learned from his pops. He sure gave up a lot to protect his dad's reputation."

"What are you talking about?" asks Rishard, walking slowly toward the young man. He feels a strong sense of urgency to get in front of his friends, as the only man in the group, the protector and all that. He's quite old-fashioned in his thoughts but well meaning.

"What? You haven't figured it all out yet?" he asks, cackling like he's high on bad marijuana.

"When Junior refused to keep giving me money from ticket sales, I threatened to make up reviews that would close down that old diner. I already had a few written—*Food poisoning from undercooked meat, pee on the toilet seats, saw the cook pick his nose*—that kind of thing." He laughs again.

From behind the door at the back of the theater, Roberta hangs her head, recalling her own threat to Pamela to spread rumors about The Northwoods Movie Theater if she didn't start choosing movies with more realistic plots. She quietly slips into the theater and ducks behind a row of chairs.

"Then good old Junior came through again, like he always has, *had*. He told me about a safe in his boss's office that held some gems, movie memorabilia from a collection that I could sell for money. That's why I'm here tonight. I thought I'd cleaned that safe out, but I realized I was missing a certificate of authenticity."

"Why do you need the certificate when you're not gettin' the knife back, since the police have it? For obvious reasons," says Vicki.

"Great question, Big Hair." Vicki narrows her eyes and imagines punching the young man in his perfectly chiseled face.

"I didn't want to give the police any help matching the knife I used with *that* knife in the safe, the one from Dane Dimoli in *Murder Meets Michigan*. They need to work a little harder than that."

"Seems silly to chance being seen in the theater. Pamela would have been able to tell the police about her collection being gone," says Yoly.

"I had plans to pay Pamela a visit. I cover my bases. Except—"

"Except you didn't expect to find a bunch of seniors sitting in the theater in the dark when you came back for that certificate." Yoly frowns as she looks at her former student.

"It's true. But ever since I lost my original key to the theater, I knew there'd be a chance someone else would find it."

"You were very careless," says Yoly. Rishard throws his arms out wide, waving Yoly and Vicki back with a wiggle of his fingers. But they don't move back. Instead, they move forward so that they are standing side-by-side in solidarity against the man. They lock arms. Vicki's phone dings. She glances down, turning April's face toward her leg.

"Ignore it," says the man.

"I…I can't. My friend is quite sick, and I always respond right away. Just give me a quick second. Vicki raises the phone so that she can read the message from Mel with Katie's contact information. "Oh my goodness!" she screams with as much gusto as she can summon. Everyone looks toward the stage where she points at the same time as she gently drops to her knees (which isn't an easy task), quickly sending Mel a text to ask her to ask Katie if Wally still tormented Junior. *URGENT!* she adds, before sending the message and looking quickly at April who mouths the words, *They're coming.* "Oh my goodness. I am so sorry about that. My friend sent me a picture of her open wound. It was something. Nobody should have to see body parts like that on their friend. Would you like to see it?" She puts her hand on the arm of a theater seat to pull herself up.

"No, that's disgusting." Of course, he'd say that. It's why he'd had to turn Junior's body over after he killed him. The blood was too much for him to stomach.

"Okay. Whew! I completely understand. Now, where were we?" Vicki and Yoly reestablish their positions on either side of Rishard. Their goal is to keep him talking and distracted until the police arrive, April's most important contribution to the Murder Movie Club to date.

"We were about to tell this young man that he's underestimating us." Rishard flexes his biceps, which bulge under the pineapples on the sleeves of his shirt, but more so from too many sweets at April's apartment, not from working out.

"That's right. I walk every day," says Yoly.

"And I stand on my feet for hours in my job. I have fantastic endurance," says Vicki. She glances toward the door, thinking she sees something move behind the last row of seats, but she can't be sure.

The young man throws his head back in laughter. "Nice try, but if a peer wasn't any competition, I highly doubt that a bunch of old people will stand in my way."

"Wally Gordon!" yells Yoly.

At the mention of his name, Wally takes a step back, nearly tripping over a seat.

"You know better than to speak to your former principal in that way. Your mother would be so disappointed."

"Ahh, you do remember me. But leave my mother out of this. She's doing just fine now that I'm paying her mortgage and sending her on trips."

"With money you didn't earn," mumbles Vicki.

"I earned it, lady, and ain't nobody gonna figure out that it was me that took out Junior Cash, so if I have to do a little more damage control to stop a bunch of old losers from interfering, then so be it."

Rishard holds Vicki back before she flies at Wally. When her phone dings again, she feigns a cramp and drops to the ground, not stopping to think how her knees might pay her back tomorrow. She quickly reads the newest message from Mel. She has excellent vision. No reading glasses needed. Satisfied with the information she needs via Mel via Katie, Vicki rises slowly.

When Wally grabs her arm, Rishard takes a swipe at him but only catches his shoulder. "Leave her alone!"

Vicki smiles, smoothing out her hair as best she can. "Well now. Sorry about that. My dear friend has a loved one caring for her now, which makes me so much happier. Family and friends are *so* important, Mr. Gordon. And we have a lot of friends and family who are going to figure this out if we come up missin'. In fact, there's even a rumor goin' round town that you've been bullyin' poor Junior since you were kids."

"So what?"

Yoly and Rishard exchange looks at they both see something move on the other side of the theater as they continue to let Vicki distract Wally.

"It seems you hold a grudge. You have to let that stuff go. It'll eat you alive—or send you to prison for life—which is exactly what's about to happen."

"What are you talking about? You're crazy! I don't have time for your blabbering."

"If only you'd had good therapy," says Yoly.

"Don't talk to me about therapy! That's a load of crap!"

Rishard adds his two cents to the conversation, the group closing in on their target. "You're clearly in a lot of pain, son."

"Stop it! All of you. Get down on the ground!" Wally smacks the baseball bat in his hand over and over again, his eyes flaring with anger. But no one moves.

"Did you ever stop to think that maybe Junior didn't mean to take your first girlfriend from you in sixth grade? That maybe *she* chose him because you're such a cad?" Vicki takes a step closer to Wally as she talks. "And how does it feel knowing that you spent the next fifteen years of your life trying to knock him down every chance you could, all because of a fragile ego over something so petty?"

"Who even remembers middle school?" Rishard says to himself.

"Shameful," Yoly says, pointing her finger at Wally.

"And then to find out that your *current* girlfriend chose Junior, too? Well, that was the last straw, wasn't it?"

"Katie deserved so much better," says Yoly.

"You keep Katie out of this! Stop it! I'm done! You're done!"

As Wally grabs Vicki by the arm again, the lights in the theater go out. The lights from the constellations in the ceiling come into view. Then, without warning to anyone, a small creature, as quiet as a mouse but with shoes at bright as Times Square, leaps onto Wally's back as she begins to claw at his face with her perfectly manicured nails.

"Oww! Oww!"

Rishard punches Wally in the stomach, this time hitting his mark. Yoly raises her leg in a way she'd only done in self-defense classes and knees her former student in the crotch. Vicki finishes Wally's attack with a strong tug of the hair on top of his head.

"Aye yi yi!" Roberta yells as she tightens her grip around Wally's neck. He thrashes his body, trying to shake Roberta free, but she's locked in with her little legs around his midline.

At the perfect time, as if in the conclusion of a mystery movie, the lights flicker on again, the loud voice of Officer Cleary declaring, "Hands up! Drop the bat!"

April smiles to herself. She places her hand on her chest, to steady her heart that's been racing for the last ten minutes, feeling both helpless to protect her friends and empowered that she'd been able to make the call to the police to explain everything. Officer Spelling had taken the call, the on-call officer for the night shift, and April had been relieved. Hearing the rage in Officer Cleary's voice now through Vicki's phone, she knows that an explanation to him might not have gone so well.

"I said, *drop the bat!* And get off his back, Ms. Kato. The rest of you, step away."

Wally looks defeated as he lets the bat slip from his fingers. As it rolls underneath each row of seats until it lands at the base of the stage under the movie screen, he makes eye contact with all of the members of the Murder Movie Club, even April, who waves from Vicki's phone. The realization of his demise hits him. The acceptance that he'd been bested my a club of movie enthusiasts is harder to come by, leaving him speechless.

Yoly puts a hand on Wally's shoulder before stepping back under Officer Cleary's direction. "You really need to learn how to forgive and forget. It's no way to live carrying a grudge for all these years."

"Thanks for the advice," he says sarcastically, lunging at his former principal one last time before Officer Cleary puts him in cuffs and hands him off to Officer Spelling to take away.

Chapter 19

"I have never been angrier than I am right now." Officer Cleary looks from Vicki to April to Yoly to Rishard to Roberta. Everyone hangs their head, accepting their chastisement, except for Roberta who meets the officer with a direct stare.

"You should be thanking us," she says defiantly. She points to her hat. "I'm a veteran. I'm your elder. And my friends and I just saved your butt by solving this crime in record time and ridding Northwoods of a tourism nightmare with ongoing negative press." She stands up on her tiptoes so that she is looking at Officer Cleary from his chin level, but she's close enough he feels her hot breath on his face. "Now. We want to hear your gratitude. *Now*."

Officer Cleary looks into the faces of the Monthly Murder Movie Club members who have now moved closer to join their compadre in crime-fighting. He's not local. He came to Northwoods to run the police department after working in New Jersey for thirteen years. Officer Cleary's been learning quickly about the workings of a small town and how thick its residents can be. He also knows when he's been defeated. Unlike Wally, he *does* know when to let go, which is exactly what he does. *Mostly*. "Thank you, Roberta. Vicki,

Yoly, Rishard, April, thank you—all of you—for helping the Northwoods Police Department to bring Wally Gordon's involvement in this crime to our attention."

"A bit more than *involvement,*" says Roberta.

"You're probably right, but we need to follow up on leads—"

"Our leads," says Rishard.

"Correct. Anyway, what I am trying to say is thank you."

"Next time you'll be nicer," says Yoly. "It seems you're being sincere. Thank you, Officer Cleary."

"Oh no. I think you may be misunderstanding something. There can be no *next time.* A murder investigation is a very serious matter, very dangerous."

"Exactly. And who better to solve murders than the Monthly Murder Movie Club?" asks Vicki.

"She's not wrong," says Yoly.

"Go home and get some rest, all of you. I'm going to clean up here for the night. I expect a visit at the station tomorrow morning, just to clarify some of the things that April told me when she called. Please bring anything you've acquired at that time."

"Definitely. We can do that," says April. "Giana will love the walk to the station. It's supposed to be warmer tomorrow morning."

"That sounds delightful," says Vicki.

"A very productive day indeed," says Yoly.

"And then maybe we can all grab lunch," says Rishard.

"I've got to put Mamo to bed. She's going to be so wired with all those extra hours on YouTube. Quit all this blabbering. Our job here is done. I'll see you nincompoops tomorrow," says Roberta as she walks down the theater aisle, stopping under the Big Dipper to wave goodbye.

"Love you, Roberta! Thanks for your service!" says Vicki.

Rishard shakes his head and rolls his eyes. But he wonders if he's been wrong about Roberta. That jump onto Wally's back was something. Quite something.

Chapter 20

The club members gather at Delish in Northwoods a week after Wally Gordon's arrest for the murder of Junior Cash. After a bit more chastising from Officer Cleary, they'd agreed to stay out of police matters and focus on the murders on the big screen instead. But though they hadn't shared their thoughts with each other, each member of the Monthly Murder Movie Club had been riding a natural high since last week and hoped that maybe—*someday*—they'd have a chance to use their sleuthing skills again.

Giana bounces on Roberta's knee, her favorite senior sleuth, which is baffling to everyone else. Rishard has put on a long sleeve Hawaiian shirt today—*who knew those even existed?*—as the first freeze warning has been issued, weeks earlier than usual. Yoly and Vicki are looking at Vicki's calendar to pick a day for Yoly to come into the salon. Vicki finally thinks she's convinced Yoly to try highlights, but Yoly doesn't care about her gray hairs one bit. She's just appeasing Vicki, who, at the moment, is trying out a new blonde wig which pairs nicely with her cranberry sweater vest. And April sits in a high back chair next to the fireplace, drinking her hot chocolate, marveling at this newfound friends' group.

The star of the hour, and the reason for the meeting outside of Monday's matinee, arrives a few minutes later. This week she's removed her braids in place of a close-to-her-head natural style, a pretty black to compliment her toffee-colored skin. She carries a cage filled with a very unhappy cat. *Angela.*

"I'm so sorry I'm late. My plane got delayed, and I needed to pick Angela up at the kennel." She talks quickly before settling into a chair around the fireplace where everyone has gathered for this meeting. "Thank you, Roberta, for finding the kennel for Angela on such short notice. She doesn't care for new circumstances. The poor thing's been through a lot."

Roberta just smiles and nods her head. She doesn't have the courage to tell Pamela that Angela had spent two nights at her condo hiding under her bed after Mamo went after her with a rolled up magazine when Angela ate all her Cheez-Its. Mamo wouldn't *really* harm her, of course, but Angela didn't know any better. It seems she'd finally met her match in Mamo, and she didn't like what she saw one bit.

Rishard hands Pamela a cup of coffee, two sugars, and a creamer packet, just the way she likes it. "Thank you so much." She takes a deep breath. "I wanted to ask you all here to thank you personally for saving Northwoods Movie Theater."

"Savin'?" asks Vicki.

Pamela holds up a hand. "Let me explain. As you've seemed to discover, thanks to the filling-in Yoly so kindly provided on the phone, I now know that Junior was stealing money for months and—"

"But not for himself," says April.

"Correct. It's true. That boy—uh, young man—didn't have a mean bone in his body. I'm sure it pained him to steal from the theater that he loved. Whatever hold Wally Gordon had over him must have been quite powerful."

"Junior was trying to keep Wally from spreading rumors about his dad's diner that would destroy their reputation and their business," says Rishard. He brushes a chocolate croissant crumb off his sleeve.

"I understand. Unfortunately, the theft happened right around the time the theater had some big bills to pay for roof repair and bathroom remodeling."

"I do love those new toilets," says Vicki.

"Good. Thanks. But just as Junior may have been trying to save his father's business, he was tanking mine. I've been sent to collections for a couple of different bills. Then

I had the idea to sell some of my movie memorabilia collection to offset the debt. I didn't want to do that. I love the items I've curated. They all come from actors or movies that mean something special to me personally or that had shown in the theater. But just as the income from ticket sales started returning to normal—after I'd asked the police to talk to Junior and Noah—I decided I might not need to sell my collection after all, if I cut back on some of my concession purchases for a bit. Anyway, unbeknownst to me, Junior had switched tactics to paying off his bully and was giving away my collection." She sighs loudly, and everyone lowers their eyes, saddened for the manager of the theater, her favorite employee and her prized collection both gone. "Dane Dimoli mailed me some of his items personally. Did I ever tell you that he's the godson of my best friend Margie?"

"No."

"That's cool."

"Wow. You're famous by association."

"What an interestin' fact."

"Maybe he'll send you another knife," says Roberta, ending the comments from the club members.

"Roberta!" everyone says in unison.

"What?" She throws her hands and feet up at the same time, almost knocking over Rishard's croissant plate.

Pamela diffuses the tension with a sweet smile. "I don't think I'll be adding any more potential weapons to my collection. But the reason why I brought you all here today is to thank you from the bottom of my heart for taking such good care of my theater. I've been very protective of what I consider to be my piece of heaven, but I know now that you all love this theater as much as I do, or else you wouldn't have spent so much time there last week after hours trying to figure out what happened to poor Junior. I still don't understand how you got inside, but I suppose you'll tell me that when you're ready." No one looks at Pamela, wanting to protect Junior's betrayal of her sacred key policy. When she realizes that no one will confess, she continues. "So, as a gift of my gratitude, I'd like to present you each with a key to the theater. Whenever you'd like to meet to discuss a movie or celebrate a life's success, or just need a safe place to chill, you're welcome to use the theater. Of course, I'm not completely crazy. I will be installing a new security system complete with cameras by the doors, so I'll know who's coming and going," she laughs uncomfortably, "but I want you to consider Northwoods Theater as your home.

Plus, you're welcome to expand the number of Monday club meetings. I'd be happy to place an order for more murder mysteries."

"That's very thoughtful, Pamela," says Yoly, accepting her key along with the rest of the clubmates. "We won't take advantage of your kind gesture."

Angela lets out a fierce meow and bats her tail against the side of her cat carrier. "I just don't know what's gotten into my kitty. She's usually so sweet and docile."

A shared look of amusement passes along the faces of Vicki, Yoly, April, Rishard, and Roberta. Even baby Giana giggles as the cat hisses. Angela is loyal only to Pamela. Time will tell how she will take to the intrusion of the Monthly Murder Movie Club members. Time will tell.

The Monthly Murder Movie Club Cozy Mystery

Book 1: Murder Movie Club (Murder on a Monday)

Book 2: Murder on a Tuesday

Book 3: Murder on a Wednesday

Murder: best served with popcorn.

That's the mantra for the members of the Monthly Murder Movie Club at The Northwoods Movie Theater. Every month, this eclectic group of northern Michigan residents gather to watch a murder mystery movie on the big screen. After stopping the projector in the middle of the movie, the members gather to discuss the crime and suspects, each making a whodunit pick before resuming the movie. *The hairdresser with the scissors? The jilted lover with poison?*

But nothing is normal on this Monday morning when the club members find the ticket-taking popcorn maker John E. Cash in the lobby of the theater, deader than any actor in their beloved movies. Using their unique talents and eccentricities, the Monthly Murder Movie Club members work collectively to solve the crime before the Northwoods Police force does. Members strive to protect the reputation of their beloved theater—and to protect their Monday meetings—because what each member is discovering is that there is so much more to their Monday club than a good old-fashioned murder mystery.

Found family, new friends, and murder investigations!

The Tucson Valley Retirement Community Cozy Mystery Series

Dying to Go (Nothing to Gush About)

Thirty-nine-year-old Rosi Laruee—named Rosisophia Doroche after her mother's beloved Golden Girls—decides that the end of her twenty-year marriage and her dad's impending knee replacement surgery are all the excuses she needs to visit Tucson Valley Retirement Community. But the drama follows Rosi when she finds the body of local tart and business owner, Salem Mansfield. The information she discovers using her newspaper reporter sleuthing skills coupled with the clues she picks up from lackluster Police Officer Dan Daniel lead to a surprise discovery when the murderer is revealed. Along the way, she meets a cast of characters in her parents' social circle who leave her questioning her parents' choices in friends while simultaneously befriending many of the residents, including a handsome landscaper and a brand-new Golden Retriever puppy she names Barley. Rosi's visit to Tucson Valley proves more than she'd bargained for, but maybe, she realizes, it's just the kind of change she needs. Laugh out loud with Rosi, and be prepared to get the happy feels along the way!

Dying to Go (Nothing to Gush About)

Dying For Wine (Seeing Red)

Dying For Dirt (All Soaped Up)

Dying to Build (Nailed It)

Dying to Dance (Cha-Cha-Ahhh)

Dying to Dink (Your Fault)

Dying Under the Big Top (Clowning Around)

Dying for Music (Hypnotic Harmony)

Dying to Wed (Double Trouble)

Dying to Go (Nothing to Gush About)
Chapter 1

I should have mailed my belongings to Tucson. I'm losing the last bit of patience that remains trying to get around boomers who crowd the moving carousel while I'm trying to retrieve two large, checked bags by myself.

I squeeze past a large gentleman with a PGA visor who is blocking my path when I see my flowered-cloth suitcase that Grandma Kate gave me when I graduated from high school. It's hard to believe that was over twenty years ago, and now I have a child that's graduated from high school, too. He'd only wanted money, though, nothing practical like luggage for all the adventures before him. This flowered piece of luggage has seen a lot of the world from a posh boutique hotel in Paris to a camping site in the wilderness in Alaska to a seaside inn in Maine. I sigh, realizing that all of those trips had included Wesley who became my husband only to become *not* my husband.

My phone beeps. I pull it out of my pocket and check the message. It's Mom.

We're here. Where are you?

I type back my response only to realize I've missed my second bag. Crap! "Excuse me. Excuse me! Can someone please grab that black bag?" I move past a couple who are talking loudly, something about the value of having a fireplace in Arizona.

A row of eyes looks back at me like I'm crazy as a line of five or six black bags scoot along the luggage carousel. "Never mind. I'll wait." I drop my eyes and walk back to my old, tattered bag and wish I'd asked for something more practical like it instead of the trendy *everyone buys black luggage* that ended up on my wedding registry all those years ago. That had been Wesley's idea, of course. The luggage got split up during the divorce, too. I got the largest piece. He got the duffle bag and laptop bag.

"Ma'am is that your bag?" asks a young woman standing next to me as I'm reminiscing and regretting in my mind all at the same time.

"Oh, yes, thanks."

She smiles. I reach for my bag.

"Here, let me get that for you." Her husband, *boyfriend?* lifts my over-the-limit bag from the belt and sets it beside my other bag.

"Thanks," I say before extending the handles of both bags and tugging them behind me. It seems as if everyone is arriving in Tucson today, probably others from the snowy Northern states like me, happy to see some sunshine.

"Ouch!" I hear from behind as I'm walking through the automatic doors. I turn around to see a middle-aged man who looks affronted and is pointing to his foot.

"Oh, sorry about that."

"Yeah, get some glasses, maybe?"

"I'll take that into consideration. Thanks," I say sarcastically.

"Rosi! Rosi! We are here!"

My mother is jumping up and down and waving her arms excitedly as she stands next to my parents' reliable Honda CRV. Dad had refused to buy something fun for himself in retirement, always the practical man, unlike many of his friends who had traded in practicality for a corvette or a refurbished '57 Chevy. "Hi, Mom."

Dad gets out of the car and insists on putting my luggage in the cargo area of the Honda though the whole reason I am here is to help out when he has his knee replacement surgery. The man can barely walk. "Hi, Rosi." He kisses me on the cheek after closing the door. "You are a sight for sore eyes," he whispers against my ear. "Your mother is driving me crazy."

"What are you two plotting?" Mom asks, grabbing my hand and pulling me to the car. "You take the front seat, Rosi. Dad will highlight attractions along the way."

Dad pats me on the knee as I take the front seat. His peppered hair is turning saltier by the year, and I touch my own brown hair, thankful that so far I've received Grandma Kate's genes and haven't started going gray. At almost forty, I have lots of friends who have been dying their hair for years. "The weather is sure nicer here this time of year than in Illinois."

"February is gorgeous in Tucson," Mom yells over the radio that is softly playing '70s classic rock as she leans forward between the two front seats.

"But there's no way you'd catch us here in the summer," says Dad. "They had twenty-five straight days last July in the three-digit temperature range. That's crazy!" He waves at a passing driver, the friendliest man I've ever known.

"We have so many plans, Rosi," says Mom. "You are going to love Tucson Valley."

"I'm not quite the demographic intended to love a retirement community, Mom."

"That's where you're wrong. There is so much to do! Plus, you're only a few years away from being able to rent a place here!"

I roll my eyes as I look out the side window at the barren landscape of the desert as we head out of Tucson and south of the city. "I'm 39."

"And at 55 you can rent your own place in Tucson Valley. It will be here before you know it!"

"Thanks for the encouragement."

"All I'm saying is that now that you are a divorcee with a kid in college, you have certain freedoms that you haven't had in the past. And maybe getting a place like we have in the desert in the middle of winter should be something to consider."

Dad turns to me and winks. "Just think, Rosi. We could be neighbors."

I smile to end this conversation. "That would be lovely." But what I really want to say is, *I'd rather eat dirt from a public park than live in a retirement community at 55 next door to my parents.*

The Ghost Texter Paranormal Cozy Mystery Series

Book 1: *Cooking to Death (Stirring the Pot)*

Twenty-four-year old Vivien Belcher—Ms. B, for obvious reasons—teaches a full class of kindergarten students in Southwest Michigan in a Lake Michigan beach town. Trying to maintain control of her overly enthusiastic students while managing life as a fully-fledged adult, Vivien's life is balancing as perfectly as a gymnast sticking her landing until the scale tips when she receives an unlikely and unwelcome text message from her ex-boyfriend…**her *dead* ex-boyfriend.**

Trapped in the Transitional World and having to atone for his many sins in life, Kasper must "make good" by helping to solve the murder of his beloved high school lunch lady. The problem? It's hard to solve a murder as a ghost. But Kasper doesn't count on Vivien's reluctance to help him, not to mention her doubt. And he *really* doesn't count on *his* reaction to Vivien moving on with relationships in her life that don't include him.

What ensues is hilarity and frustration as Kasper's time is running out to convince Vivien to help him. Being a ghost is hard. But so is being a new teacher.

Cooking to Death (Stirring the Pot)

Dribbling to Death (Taking His Shot)

Haunting to Death (Taking the Wheel)

The Secret of Blue Lake (1)

The only true certainty in life is dying, but there's a whole lot of life to live from beginning to end if you're lucky. When Chicago news reporter Meg Popkin's dad makes a surprise move to a tiny town called Blue Lake, Michigan, in the middle of nowhere and away from his family after losing his wife to cancer, she wonders if there is more to the move than *just a change of scenery*. With the help of a new, self-confident reporter at the station, Brian Welter, she tries to figure out what the secret attraction to Blue Lake is for its many new residents and along the way discovers that maybe she's been missing out on some of the joys of living herself.

Drama, mystery, and romance abound for Meg as she learns about love, loss, and herself.

The Secret of Silver Beach (2)

After solving the mystery of the secret of Blue Lake, Meg returns to Chicago and to her new job as co-host on Chicago Midday. But when poor chemistry with Trenton Dealy leads to problems on the show, Meg is assigned a travel segment that will send her on location all around Lake Michigan visiting beach towns and local tourist attractions. The trip takes her away from fiancé Brian who has to continue anchoring the nightly news in Chicago. When odd threats start hurtling in Meg's direction, she finally confesses to Brian and those closest to her that she might have a stalker. Do the threats have something to do with the new information she learned about her dad's past in the little town of St. Joseph, Michigan, or is there something bigger at play that threatens more than Meg's livelihood?

Marcy Blesy is the author of over thirty books including the popular cozy mystery series: The Tucson Valley Retirement Community Cozy Mystery Series, a hilarious misadventure in amateur sleuthing. Her adult romance mystery series includes The Secret of Blue Lake and The Secret of Silver Beach, set in Michigan. The Ghost Texter Paranormal Cozy Mystery Series, featuring a sleuthing kindergarten teacher in Michigan was recently released. Children's books include the best-selling Be the Vet series along with the following early chapter book series: Evie and the Volunteers, Niles and Bradford, Third Grade Outsider, and Hazel, the Clinic Cat.

Marcy enjoys searching for treasures along the shores of Lake Michigan. She's still waiting for the day when she finds a piece of red beach glass.

Marcy is a believer in love and enjoys nothing more than making her readers feel a book more than simply reading it.

I would like to extend a heartfelt thanks to Betty for being the first person to read my cozy mysteries and for giving me her guidance and expertise as my editor. To my ARC team: YOU ROCK! Your encouragement and kindness is so appreciated. You know how to put a smile on a girl's face. Thank you.

Thank you to Ed, Connor, and Luke for always championing my dreams.